NO MATTER WHEN

BW Vilakazi

Translated from isiZulu by Nkosinathi Sithole

OXFORD
UNIVERSITY PRESS
SOUTH AFRICA

OXFORD
UNIVERSITY PRESS

Oxford University Press is a department of the University of Oxford.
It furthers the University's objective of excellence in research, scholarship,
and education by publishing worldwide. Oxford is a registered trade mark of
Oxford University Press in the UK and in certain other countries.

Published in South Africa by
Oxford University Press Southern Africa (Pty) Limited

Vasco Boulevard, Goodwood, N1 City, P O Box 12119, Cape Town,
South Africa

Noma Nini was originally published in isiZulu by Mariannhill Mission Press in 1935. This
translation is of the fourth edition, published in 1962.

The moral rights of the translator have been asserted.

First published 2018

No Matter When

ISBN 978 0 19 073791 7 (print)
ISBN 978 0 19 073871 6 (ebook)

First impression 2018

Typeset in Utopia Std 10.5pt on 15.5pt
Printed on 70gsm woodfree paper

Acknowledgements
Co-ordinator at the Centre for Multilingualism and Diversities Research, UWC: Antjie Krog
Publisher: Helga Schaberg
Project manager: Liz Sparg
Editor: Mary Reynolds
Book and cover designer: Judith Cross
Illustrator: James Berrangé
Typesetter: Aptara Inc.
Printed and bound by: Academic Press

We are grateful to the following for permission to reproduce photographs: Shutterstock/
Ollyy/125120741 (cover); Museum Africa (p. x); OUPSA/Admire Kanhenga (p.169).

The authors and publisher gratefully acknowledge permission to reproduce copyright
material in this book. Every effort has been made to trace copyright holders, but if any
copyright infringements have been made, the publisher would be grateful for information
that would enable any omissions or errors to be corrected in subsequent impressions.

THIS BOOK FORMS part of a series of eight texts and a larger translation endeavour undertaken by the Centre for Multilingualism and Diversities Research (CMDR) at the University of the Western Cape (UWC). The texts translated for this series have been identified time and again by scholars of literature in southern Africa as classics in their original languages. The translators were selected for their translation experience and knowledge of a particular indigenous language. Funding was provided by the National Institute for the Humanities and Social Sciences (NIHSS) as part of their Catalytic Research Programme. The project seeks to stimulate debate by inserting neglected or previously untranslated literary texts into contemporary public spheres, providing opportunities to refigure their significance and prompting epistemic changes within multidisciplinary research. Every generation translates for itself. Within the broad scope of several translation theories and the fact that every person translates differently from the next, it is hoped that these texts will generate further deliberations, translations and retranslations.

NATIONAL INSTITUTE
FOR THE HUMANITIES
AND SOCIAL SCIENCES

UNIVERSITY *of the*
WESTERN CAPE

Centre for Multilingualism
and Diversities Research

Introduction

BW Vilakazi was not only a novelist and a poet but also a notable scholar, at home in English and isiZulu. He wrote his academic papers and theses in English, but chose to write his imaginative work – his fiction and poetry – in isiZulu. It is my belief that he and his contemporaries who were writing in African languages anticipated the well-known debates about language choice, particularly in the context of colonisation, that Chinua Achebe and Ngugi wa Thiong'o brought to an international arena decades later.

While I am not concerned with what language African writers should write in, I am, as Vilakazi was, concerned about the marginality of African languages and their literatures, and I hope that he would be pleased to see his novel – so widely acclaimed in his own language – finally made accessible to a much wider audience. I believe that if he had lived longer he would have translated this fine book himself.

Vilakazi's novel takes place when missionaries and their supposedly civilising mission had taken root in Natal (now KwaZulu-Natal), and when a clash of cultures was taking place. As historians have noted, missionaries in South Africa intended to "civilise" the natives by remaking them: changing their beliefs, traditions and customs, values, way of life and means of livelihood. It was this task that they took upon themselves that ended up dividing the African community between the Kholwa (converts) and the so-called heathens. Those who converted received the education provided by the missionaries and this led to most of them rejecting African culture, while others tried to negotiate their place between the two opposing cultures.

But while converts willingly rejected uneducated Africans and distanced themselves from their precolonial roots, they found that they could not be admitted to the life of the whites that they aspired to. The result was a sense of not belonging for this African elite group: they fitted neither the African nor the Western way of life.

Among the most notable of the Kholwa was John Langalibalele Dube, founder of the isiZulu-English newspaper, *ILanga lase Natal*, first president of the South African Native National Congress (later, the African National Congress) and founder of Ohlange Institute – a school where Vilakazi taught in 1933. The manner in which this class of natives was alienated from other Africans is epitomised in a speech that Dube gave in 1911 to celebrate the arrival of the missionaries in South Africa and thank them for the better life they had brought to the Kholwa. The speech shows how the missionaries had succeeded in changing the way of life of African people like Dube, and how his class looked down upon those who still clung to their traditional ways:

Go into a native Christian home. It was a humble dwelling, but it had a door which swung on its hinges, and through which a man might walk erect as became his dignity, and there was a window or two to let in the light of heaven, and ... a bed to sleep upon, and a table to eat from, and chairs to sit upon, and a book or two to read; and last, not least, all livestock was harboured outside. (Laughter and applause.) All humble and plain, but compare it with the hut of a heathen, into which one must crawl like a reptile, to sit on the floor in the darkness along with goats on the one side and calves on the other; with no other furniture than divers evil-smelling things in the hinder portion of the building. Who was it that taught this cleaner and more comfortable life? Who was it that taught the decency and the benefits of wearing clothes? (*Christian Express* 1 August 1911: 116-117).

It is in the polarised environment discernible in Dube's speech, of a society divided between the Kholwa and the heathens, that *No Matter When* is set. Thomas, who is raised and groomed by the missionary Mr Grout, is a Kholwa, and he makes it clear to Nomkhosi (the main character of the story and his fiancée) that he and she are worlds apart from the heathens. Thomas represents the class of the aspiring, an educated, proud young man who has preached for Mr Grout. Since most girls are not educated like him, even Grout does not see any girl suitable for Thomas until Nomkhosi arrives and learns Western ways from them. Mr Grout represents the missionaries described above and is based on a real character, Aldin Grout, who founded a mission near the mouth of the Mvoti River, a place later named Groutville. It was in Groutville that Vilakazi himself was raised, as was the Nobel Peace Prize winner, Albert Luthuli, who is likely to have influenced Vilakazi's faith in the possibility of blending African and Western cultures.

Grout was a benevolent man who did much for the people around him, and he not only helped the Kholwa, but the heathen as well. His home became a station where people coming from or going to Durban from Zululand and other places could rest, be fed and spend the night, to resume their journeys the following day.

While the missionary in the novel does his work for God and black people with the utmost sincerity, the product of his labour is not always positive, as we see in the character of Thomas. Though Thomas is educated and a Kholwa, he is not a character that we are supposed to like. Through Thomas, Vilakazi distances himself from people like Dube and the position he expressed in 1911.

It is Nsikana who is an exemplary character and with whom we identify. We want him to win in the end because we know Thomas is bad despite being a Kholwa and having lived his life in Grout's mission. Thomas is a cruel overseer. He is promiscuous and has an affair with Nomkhosi's adoptive sister, Ntombinjani. The manner in which he courts her (secretly, and squeezing her hand to make her agree to his proposal from pain) shows that he goes against the grain of Christian living: he is a hypocrite. The final irony is that he resorts to witchcraft when he realises that he is losing Nomkhosi and is overcome by jealousy. Nsikana does not have these flaws. What makes him even more agreeable is that he manages to live in both the world of the non-believers and that of the Kholwa. Having gone to school for a while and later worked in Durban, he is a Kholwa, but still fits in well with traditionalists. Vilakazi tells us that "In the land of his people [Nsikana] dressed like the heathens if they were going to traditional functions" (page 108). The authorial voice elaborates in a way that defends Nsikana, at the same time presenting this statement as the argument of the novel itself:

> He could not have done otherwise, for it was necessary to show that even though he behaved like a white man, he had not completely jettisoned the ways of his own people; not like today when some people claim to be following the whites but they cannot fit into the life of whites, and then they say they are black but know nothing about blacks. (page 108)

The contrast between Thomas and Nsikana is especially marked on two points. Firstly, as we have seen, Thomas is unfaithful to Nomkhosi; Nsikana, in contrast, refuses the suggestion by his sister, Nokuthela, that he marry more than one wife.

Nokuthela and Nsikana engage in a debate about polygamy, one of the main bones of contention between Africans and missionaries. The missionaries wanted to get rid of polygamy as much as they wanted to do away with African song and dance and reverence for the ancestors. In allowing Nokuthela and Nsikana to argue about this, Vilakazi echoes the missionaries' claim that there was no force in their endeavours to civilise black people, but all was done through a peaceful conversation. While Vilakazi rejects some of the missionaries' ideas like the prohibition of ululating at weddings, he seems to support their view on polygamy. As Bhekizizwe Peterson observes, "Vilakazi himself, like numerous others among the African elite, was adamant that Africans needed to progress, in Dube's words, beyond 'the abyss of antiquated tribal systems'. This meant that retrospective practices, such as polygamy, had to be jettisoned but it did not mean the wholesale rejection of traditional practices" (2000: 97).

Thus the debate staged in the novel ends with Nsikana and his position against polygamy winning the day. But polygamy is given a fair voice, as we hear the girls discussing Thomas's affair with Ntombinjani: they argue that it is better to be one of several wives than to be made a fool of by a man "thinking you are the only wife, while there are others more important than you who take from him what they want" (page 120).

Secondly, the text imagines a South Africa where different races, black and white, can live together harmoniously and in mutual respect. This is seen in the conversations in Durban where Nsikana has worked, where young black men sit outside in the evenings with whites and discuss many things on equal terms, with their employer–servant relationship put on the back-burner. Here the text is relevant for us today, as we in South Africa battle to find a non-racial nation 24 years after the end of apartheid. What the text suggests is needed is mutual tolerance and respect for each other's cultures, and openness to learning from the good in cultures other than one's own. It is telling that when the missionary and his wife are struggling to find a solution to the love triangle between Nomkhosi, Nsikana and Thomas, they decide to seek an indigenous solution by calling Makhwatha (Nomkhosi's father) and letting the matter be decided through his senior daughter, Nontula. In other words: Vilakazi removes his story from the oversimplified binaries of Kholwa and uneducated, Christian and traditional, and creates a space in which choices and agency are shown in their complex reality.

Racial intolerance still informs our new South Africa despite the bright promises of liberation and reconciliation, and one wonders how Vilakazi would feel about it if he were alive today. Perhaps some would find his ideas simplistic, but I believe that even today imagining a peaceful and harmonious life for all the races in the country can never be wrong, though black people (and whoever is marginalised) have every right to feel tired and angry.

Dr Nkosinathi Sithole
University of the Western Cape, Cape Town
June 2018

References

Peterson, B (2000) *Monarchs, Missionaries, and African Intellectuals.* Johannesburg: University of the Witwatersrand Press.

Peterson, B (2012) "Black writers and the historical novel." In: David Attwell and Derek Atridge (Eds) *The Cambridge History of South African Literature.* Cape Town: Cambridge University Press.

Benedict Wallet Vilakazi (1906–1947)

Benedict Vilakazi has been described as the father of Nguni literature. He was born at the Groutville Mission Station in 1906. His mother, Leah Hlongwane Vilakazi, was the sister of the Right Reverend J Mdelwa Hlongwane ka Mnyaziwezulu. His maternal grandmother was the sister of Queen Ngqambuza, a wife of Mpande kaCetshwayo. At birth, Vilakazi was named Bambatha kaMshini after his father, Mshini kaMakhwatha.

His parents were Christian converts, and he attended the local mission school at Groutville until he was ten years old. The mission station had been established in the 1840s by the missionary Aldin Grout, and it is the setting for much of this novel. Vilakazi moved on to a Roman Catholic secondary school, St. Francis College, in Mariannhill, Durban. In 1923, Vilakazi gained a teaching certificate and started teaching, first at Mariannhill, and then at a seminary in Ixopo.

While working at the Ohlange Institute near Durban, he began academic studies and was awarded a BA degree from the University of South Africa in 1934, and Honours from the University of the

Witwatersrand (Wits) for his work in Bantu Studies in 1935. A year later, Vilakazi was employed by the Wits Bantu Studies department. There he and CM Doke, the head of the department, began developing a dictionary that, now in its fourth edition, is still regarded as the most authoritative dictionary of its kind. Vilakazi became the first black South African teacher of white South African students at university level.

Vilakazi published a number of literary works during his life. His first novel, *Noma Nini* (1935), was the first in isiZulu to deal with modern issues and is a classic exploration of a Christianised African elite who are caught between African and Western modes of living. But it is done "in a manner that shows the personal and social consequences that flow from the contending social groups, cosmologies and epistemologies in ways that challenge the usual notions of 'tradition' and 'modernity', 'collaboration' and 'resistance'" (Bhekizizwe Peterson, *Cambridge History of South African Literature*, p. 305).

His first poetry anthology, *Inkondlo KaZulu* (1939), merged European rhyme and stanza forms with the very different style of traditional praise poetry in isiZulu, izibongo. Scholars have also praised the beautiful and poignant descriptions of landscape, the vivid sense of place he captured in both prose and verse. Other publications include: *UDingiswayo KaJobe* (1939), *Nje Nempela* (1944) and *Amal'eZulu* (1945).

In 1946, Vilakazi earned a PhD for his academic work, "The Oral and Written Literature in Nguni," the first PhD to be awarded to a black South African. Only a year after this momentous occasion, he died of meningitis at the age of forty-one.

BW Vilakazi was awarded the Order of Ikhamanga – Gold posthumously, for "his exceptional contribution to the field of literature in indigenous languages and the preservation of isiZulu culture."

Main characters

Makhwatha: Nomkhosi's father, of Mzwangedwa
Nomkhosi: daughter of Makhwatha
Nontula: Nomkhosi's official eldest sister
Ntombinjani: Nomkhosi's half-sister from Phikiwe's house
Nsikana Mbokazi: son of Bhoqo from Nkobongo area; suitor of Nomkhosi
Nokuthela: Nsikana's sister
Nkomeni and **Smonqo:** friends of Nsikana
Nongunyaza: half-brother and enemy of Nsikana
Thomas: son of Nogiyela from the Qwabe area; suitor of Nomkhosi
Mfundisi: Minister Grout, minister at the mission station at Groutville
Sihlangusinye: diviner at Msizini
Ndosi: driver living at Groutville

Zulu leaders who were historical figures before and at about the time in which the novel is set

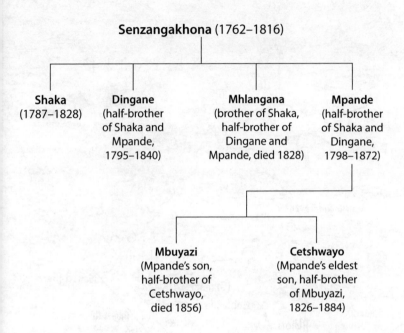

Senzangakhona (1762–1816)

Shaka
(1787–1828)

Dingane
(half-brother
of Shaka and
Mpande,
1795–1840)

Mhlangana
(brother of Shaka,
half-brother of
Dingane and
Mpande, died 1828)

Mpande
(half-brother
of Shaka and
Dingane,
1798–1872)

Mbuyazi
(Mpande's son,
half-brother of
Cetshwayo,
died 1856)

Cetshwayo
(Mpande's eldest
son, half-brother
of Mbuyazi,
1826–1884)

KwaZulu-Natal of *No Matter When*

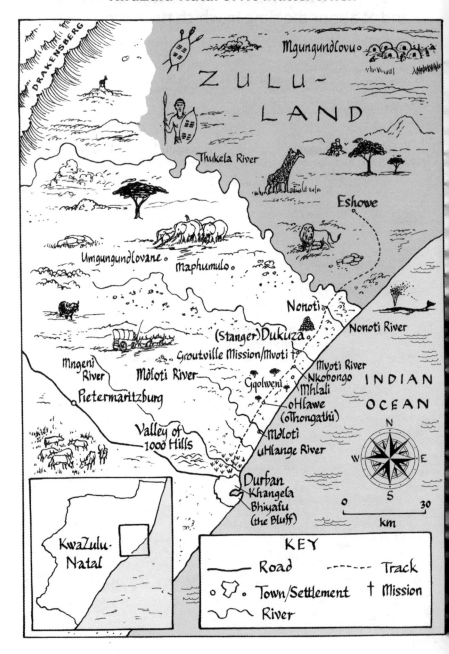

NO MATTER WHEN

BW Vilakazi

I dedicate this book to *MBONGENI* and *SIPHIWE*:
Nomasomi's sons

Foreword

Dr BW Vilakazi died tragically towards the end of 1947. By that time, he was a powerful writer. Six years have passed since his passing away, but the remembrance of his dedication and his enthusiasm for the development of his people is still a fire that burns in many people's hearts. Even the fact that this short novel of his – *Noma Nini* – needs to be reprinted, is testament that his motivation is still felt regarding the writing of books in isiZulu. It pleases me a great deal to see this.

As this book is re-published, thanks should go to Mr CLS Nyembezi, MA, who revised it, especially with regard to its structure. I am sure that this will add to the excitement of those who will read it.

CM Doke
University of the Witwatersrand
Johannesburg

Preface

This story that I am writing in this book today is a story I was told by my father when I was very young. But here, I am not writing it as it was told to me because it would be very short and not satisfy anybody. My father's telling created a space for this story, which includes the characters of Nomkhosi and Nsikana. These people did indeed live at Mvoti at some point. It is also true that Nomkhosi had been found when people were running away from the war. But the truth of this story ends there.

Most of what I have written are things I have taken from here and there, and put together to spice up my story, to make it interesting and readable. That Minister Grout in this story had a wife when he started the mission at Mvoti is one of the things I have created, as we all know that the minister's wife had by that time already been killed by TB. She died when they were still at eBhayi, and she never saw the Zulus.

Through this novel I intend to add a drop to the books that have been written by us, the Zulu people, like those of Fuze, Mafukuzela (JL Dube), Dlomo, Mpanza, Zungu, Ntuli, Mdonswa, Mdladla, Mbatha, and others whom I don't even know of. I hope that this book, too, will add value, as *Inkondlo KaZulu*, which I published last year, did.

This book won the competition run by the International Institute of African Languages and Cultures in London in 1933. When it returned – having been the only one to win, others earning consolation prizes – I revised it for publication as you see it now.

For its publication, I am grateful to the monastery in Mariannhill, for taking this novel and promising to publish it and cover the costs of publication themselves. That means a lot to me. I am very grateful to the school's inspector, Mr. Malcolm, who read the whole book after it came back from overseas, when it was still in my handwriting; he pointed to some areas of the novel that needed changing and even went so far as to find other white people who were prepared to take it (for publication), if I did not agree with the publishers in Mariannhill. This has given me strength to write another book in the future.

I now thank my wife, MaNxaba, with whom I always shared what I had written, and she would criticise what was not written well, and offer her advice on other things, until this book became what it is.

BWV
Groutville
28 January 1935

Nomkhosi of my father

I love you for your blackness,
which is like the beginning of night,
which lightens up cats' eyes:
those eyes are yours, Nomkhosi.

I love you for your chest,
which feeds my siblings,
the milk whiter than snow:
the snow is your beauty, Nomkhosi.

I love you when you speak
as if you are tired and don't want to,
your eyes moving inside you
in the shadows of long eyelashes.

I see the beauty of maidens
from Zululand who are long forgotten
and dead; I see it striking
like lightning hidden by the mountains.

Your firm steps as you walk
tire a young man courting.
He passes you and then takes a glance backwards,
watches you and tears flow.

I love you for the hair on your head,
a black mamba of the forest
with monkey-ropes coiled around its body.
It shines like fat.

I love your teeth with their gap.
They adorn your mouth like an arum lily
of the pools of the waters of uThukela:
as if you don't eat at all.

I love you for your hands,
which look like they touch no hoe.
They bathe Nandi's children
who bloom with beauty like you.

Everyone loves you for all that is yours;
I worship you as though
you were not born on earth
but descended in heaven's basket.

1

The land was still peaceful. Men from the upper echelons of power in Zululand sat basking in the sun at Mgungundlovu. There were Mondise, son of Jobe; Ndlela, son of Sompisi, who was Dingane's senior induna; Lunguza, son of Mpukane; Sivivi, son of Maqungo; and other people of importance. In order to avoid their conversation being overheard, they moved to a special hut next to the warriors' huts. The warriors were away on an offensive battle.

Mondise says: "You see, men, there's a new hand in leadership today; things are not going as they did before. I want to understand what is causing disunity in the Zulu kingdom. Even as I speak I'm apprehensive, lest one of you report on me, and I end up being stitched to the sleeping mat by the spear."

Lunguza responds: "It's they of the senior induna group who should tell us why they allow the King to run amok."

"That's true, you son of Mpukane. Tell us, Ndlela, tell us what's happening here," says Sivivi.

It is Mondise who responds: "I'm scared because I was there at Dukuza when King Dingane killed his brother while the warriors were jovially performing the ukugiya dance, not aware that Dingane had conspired with his brothers. At first, the Zulus said: 'Oh, no, it's an accident. Why would King Senzangakhona's son kill his brother without any provocation?' The wise men appeared only recently when this Dingane, who now doesn't care about us any more, had already assumed power. These wise men appeared and asked Mhlangana what had happened, and he explained the whole thing to them."

"Didn't you hear that when Dingane stabbed Mhlangana at the fence of the homestead, Mhlangana exposed him, laying bare all his malevolent acts?"

"What did he say?" Ndlela, son of Sompisi, asks.

"He said the spear that came from above – as we were told – was released purposely by Dingane so that it would fall on Shaka's chest, and he would fall right there and never rise again. Remember that when it was suggested that the dance should stop because King Shaka had been wounded, Dingane, Mbopha and Mhlangana said the King was not wounded, and the dancing should continue?"

"Yes, we see," say the others.

Sivivi continues: "It is known that before he died on the day after he was stabbed, Shaka called his brothers to the hut early in the morning. He called them in the presence of the others who were listening and cursed them, referring to the white birds that were coming to conquer the Zulu, rule them and turn them into slaves. Is it not true that Shaka said the whites would arrive, that he saw them approaching through the water, and that his brothers would never rule?"

All are dead quiet, as if someone has physically shut their mouths; but they are engrossed in their thoughts, all contemplating Dingane's leadership capabilities.

Then Ndlela speaks: "Now I see, as you yourselves do, why the King ruthlessly murdered the Boers. Yes, Zulu, you are spot on, I also do not know what will become of me in this troubled kingdom."

"If you, Ndlela, are doubtful and scared, you who are milking the udder of the cow of the Zulus, what about the rest of us?" asks Lunguza.

"You say so, Lunguza, because there is something that you don't know," answers Ndlela. "Didn't you hear that when the King killed his brothers and exiled those who were wailing for Shaka, I protected Mpande? I said he should not be killed, because he is a weakling."

"Yes, son of Sompisi, we know that you protected him. You even said that since he was the one who has children, he needn't be killed, and also because he is a moron and won't try to take over the kingship," says Mondise.

"But even you, son of Sompisi, could see that Mpande had his own hidden agenda; he is fat inside like a wild mousebird," says one of those listening. "Why is it that while we are here, he's rumoured to be in the white man's land, and who knows who else he meets there but the whites?"

"No, you are mistaken, Zulu, if you say that I am close to Mpande, because my only intention was to prevent Senzangakhona's house from being completely wiped out," says Ndlela.

Sivivi says: "Well, I actually believe that you *could* see the hidden agenda, son of Sompisi, because one always found you talking with Mpande. Is it not you who accompanied him and left him near Nyezane? You deliberately did not go through to the Thukela River because you feared Dingane's izinduna, his headmen patrolling along it, looking for spies transporting news about the Zulus to the whites. We also know that you are responsible for the triumph of Mpande's army over that of Dingane at Maqongqo."

"Oh my men, why are you talking like this? Don't you know that the King doesn't even look me in the eyes any more? Even when I'm summoned, and I declaim his praises, he just remains unmoved. Even his drinking pot for amasi, the one I used to lick, today it is given to the likes of Malambule. Ever since the king's army lost at Maqongqo, I've not been well emotionally," Ndlela says, taking a bit of snuff and smoking.

Ndlela gazes far away, as if through his mind different epochs are passing. He sees himself and remembers: there was a time when he, as a boy, would look at Shaka's warriors and wish one day to be a greater warrior than any of them could ever be. By this time he was a carrier of sleeping mats, hemp pipes and dagga for the uDibi regiment. He also realises the consequences of forsaking Dingane and conspiring with Mpande. Why, Mpande was not even a king! He saw the two sides attacking each other at the battle of Maqongqo near uPhongolo, and how he, for his part, had not wanted Dingane's side to win, even though he was Dingane's induna.

And since then, all the rumours that had spread among the Zulu people – how he, Ndlela, was responsible for the loss of the battle of Maqongqo, because he had strategised his attack so badly – had reached him. He wonders whether that talk has also already reached the ears of the King. All this runs through his mind in seconds, and then suddenly he hears the other headmen hailing: "Bayede! You of Heaven!" They hail the King at the exact time that Ndlela is busy releasing some bladder-water at the fence, so he finds himself hailing the King alone after the others have finished; and his voice sounds like that of a goat stranded alone in the wild, a goat crying in the middle of the night. Dingane looks at him with piercing eyes. He does not blink, but asks: "Ndlela, son of Sompisi, I ask you, my induna; I say about Maqhoboza:

Stabber of the rain
Leather bag of men and cattle,
Field-marker, he's marking it for himself;
Goer-down his own path alone,
Stabber of the cowards

Where is he? I ask you, and where are the others?"

Ndlela begins trembling, stuttering, and does not know how to answer because the King comes from nowhere with this question and takes him unawares. When he tries to respond, "Bayede e...e...e," the King cuts him off:

"And these men you are with here, you also want to make them desert me and join my brother Mpande? I ask you, son of Sompisi, what is Mpande doing in the white man's land? When you parted with him near Nyezane, after escorting him with some of my warriors, what did he say to you?"

Ndlela is so terrified that he falls down. He realises that the King knows about him and Mpande. For a long time he just lies there, and not one of the people are thinking of fetching water to pour on him and raising him to his feet. After a long while he staggers upright and says, "You-of-the-Reed[1], what have I done, being your slave as I am?" But again, Dingane cuts him off:

"You Lunguza, son of Mpukane, and you Sivivi of Maqungo, take this man away and come back to tell me that the dog has coughed his last cough."

That was how Ndlela's end happened. But the King was not satisfied by Ndlela's death. He summoned the council to Mgungundlovu – which was rumoured to be built with fighting sticks reddened by the blood of young men! He ordered that everybody of Ndlela's house, as well as the warriors who lost the battle at Maqongqo, be rounded up and killed. He wanted only those who loved him, the King, to remain in Zululand. The men dispersed to report the order to the others, to sharpen their spears and shake out the dirt from their shields, because tonight all those involved in Mpande's desertion would be wiped out.

But people do not flow one way like water. Some went directly to warn those who were to be killed. They advised them to run away when dusk was falling. Some of the warriors followed Mpande's example and ran to the white man's land. Some were afraid to run straight to the mouth of the Thukela River, and instead, they went in the direction of Umgungundlovane[2], thus hiding their tracks. They hoped to join Mpande across the Thukela, and if he had already left by then, they would follow on his heels.

When Zulus run away, they tend to attack those they come across, to prevent others from thinking that everybody who runs is a coward. So all the smaller nations that were living along the south were stabbed and killed, or chased and forced to cross the Thukela.

When those who were running away had crossed the Thukela, they chased and attacked those at Sithundu, and at Nonoti and at Mthandeni and at Makhovana, and went on to Madundube. They went down the upper part of the Mvoti River near the Hlimbithwa, until they stabbed the sea sands.

There was no construction in the land at that time. There were no roads. The land was full of forests. If you go to these places even today, you will find many hills, cut here and there by the small rivers joining the Mvoti and Thukela. Then there were wild areas stretching far, where no vegetable grew except for the climbing gourd and monkey orange trees. There were mimosa trees, which do not grow that tall, allowing the goats and wild animals to eat them. In these places, when the sun rose and the sand got hot, and you were tired and resting under the tree with your shield lying next to you, you would hear the tree-cricket chirruping, hear grasshoppers and the tree frog announcing the heat. This was where the Valley of a Thousand Hills threw its bushy tail for the last time. The land in the south was a vast open land, a plain, and there were forests inhabited by green and black mambas. There were hills everywhere. Rock snakes peeled off their skin every summer to expand their bodies so that they could swallow even bigger prey that slithered through these places. No one was brave enough to walk alone there; even today, though the roads have been built, you will twitch with fear and be unable to sleep if you hear the stories from there.

These places were frequented by the underground people, the tokoloshes. One of them once met a man running away from the war and asked him, "Where did you see me?"

The Zulu man said, "I just saw you now."

But immediately after he had spoken, the tokoloshe, the one in front of him, slapped him with the outside of the hand, and the man lost his speech. When he turned to go, it said to him: "If you meet us next time and we ask you 'Where did you see us?' you must say 'I saw you coming from very, very far'".

When the herbalists had cured the man, he told this story to others.

When you spoke in these hills your words echoed, as if many voices were speaking, like the voices of the baboons and the monkeys coming back from stealing mealies. If you were standing on top of the Madundube mountain, where those of the Mlawu of Khuzwayo live today, you would see below you the long line of the Mvoti's sliding clear water, flowing towards the sea; and the black forests surrounding a number of hills; and the green fields of sugar cane belonging to the Kholwa, the believers, spreading like the blanket thrown over the white man's sleeping mat, the bed. And far away in the north, where the Zulu warriors came as they were fleeing from Dingane, you saw the waters of uThukela breathing sadly, and all the trees of the forests moving, which had always moved as they move today; and uThukela still flowing to fill the sea, but the sea never gets full.

Men ran away; women ran away; young men ran away and young women ran away; and you too, child, started with your legs behind those of your mother. If you got tired, you were left there and then. As for you, men, your love would end there, because how could you remember your wife? And you, young man, how could you remember your girlfriend and protect her, when you had seen the spear sparkling, and the blood red in front of you? Remember that a man becomes an animal in the face of killing. And sometimes when they do return, some are killed by the insanity that is caused by killing people, and by wounds that never heal. This is what caused our forefathers to migrate down here and forget about the civilisation and knowledge they had been born to, born for, in far-away lands in the north, where instead of rivers there are lakes.

They crossed the drifts over uThukela at a run. And then there was this one night: the moon was full, the sky clear with no clouds. As it came from the east, the moon was white and round, vying with the stars over whose sparkling was most supreme. Even the bodies and souls of the people were infused by some sort of epiphany. It was on this very night that on top of the Ntumeni Hill a young woman was heard singing with a soft voice. She was singing the song of the men of Mzwangedwa. There was no one to support her singing:

Agree, the young men's spear is down,
With the beast of Ngwababane.
You were not there Mashiya-Nkomo.
Agree, the young men's spear is down.

Those who heard her listened in astonishment. They kept quiet and listened to her until she stopped singing and succumbed to her own moods. As she became quiet, the oxen bellowed, the cows lowed and their calves responded in their kraals. The dogs barked far away, as if they were scaring the witches away. The cocks were misled into thinking it was dawn, and they crowed, making so much noise that they were heard in all the villages of Ntubeni. Perhaps their noise joined together, and who knows, went all the way to the white man's land – things like these cannot be understood. The wind was fresh, fitting the state of the stars and moon. And the tree-crickets of the soil chirped, thanking their god for the food they had received that day. In short, everything was joyful, relishing its existence on earth. There is a saying that if animals are making such noises, it means trouble is looming. And as for the dogs, to this day it is believed that if the dogs howl, then someone will die in those homesteads. If the cattle low at the same time and it is full moon, it means war is looming. Those who have babies, and the cripples, and those who are sick are all pitied, because they are the ones left behind when people flee that night. By the time they wake up it is all quiet, there will be hunger and nobody to hear their cries.

Then on the following night, at midnight, the crying of the women clasping their heads was heard. It was the terrifying cry of someone who no longer can free herself, being devoured by a wild animal which has started with her head. The footsteps of the men and young men were all over the mountains. Some were saying, "It is here!" Others cried, "The battle has begun; happy are those who are in the forefront. May you taste it for me! I will tell my mother and the girls at home about it."

In the Qwabe homesteads near Ntubeni, the sons of Mzimba and Hlonono ran away:

Dlomo grows by day to us, Mayangeni,
Dlomo of the Mhlathuze area, Big Nondaba.
The Head-shaker who's no he-goat,
He eats mimosa trees and leans on cat-thorn trees.
Jaundiced red-mouthed vulture,
Equal to the heifers of his maternal home.

Curve-backed one who is equal to Nqumela, equal to Ngqeshe,
Mavundla, son of Lugoloza,
You of the king's horse,
The horse that was lost for years,
It came back home carrying a foal
Mhlongo the great one, Mhlongo, son of Ngqeshe.

Some ran the whole night without sleep. Two of them were members of iMboza regiment, Makhwatha of Govu and Bantukabezwa of Mvuyane, a very dark and bald old man. They travelled through forests and crossed rivers. Not one among them knew where their wives had run to. When they were separated, they advised their wives and children to flee toward the white man's land, to cross to the north of uMvoti as the warriors were chasing the men who ran toward the south.

When it was morning, they saw the buildings of Shaka's homestead, Dukuza, which were identifiable from afar by their white yards. When the sun was up and they were closer to Dukuza, they sat down at Mbazamo below the fig trees, the cat-thorn trees and the thorn trees of the coastal thorn-veld. They started talking, and asked each other about the food they carried for the journey. They began to smoke. Suddenly they saw a small bundle of cloth near them that seemed to have dropped from the trees. They approached it carefully, thinking it might be an evil token, but when they got closer, found it was a baby girl left there with a gourd with some milk-gruel, some finely crushed boiled mealies, and the skin used to carry a child.

Bantukabezwa said: "What are we to do with this child? Whose is it anyway?"

Makhwatha answered: "It's as though I know her. Doesn't she belong to Mthembu's son?"

As he knew the sons of Mthayi of Lubhozo of the baThembu clan well, Bantukabezwa said: "No, my brother, it is not, let's go, lest we touch that which should not be touched; perhaps it's evil magic."

It was difficult for Makhwatha. He had already taken his shield and weapons and was turning to go when suddenly he heard her cry. It prompted thoughts of his own children whom he had left the previous day; he was not sure if he would ever see them again. His face was filled with shame; he took the child and lifted her onto his shoulders, as if she was his own child. He took his spears, assegai and shield, and quickly ran further as the army was reported to be closing in on them. They arrived at Dukuza and put the traditional stones on the cairn. They moved on to the old gravesite in Dukuza, where they spent some time remembering the ancestors. They praised Shaka, talking to his bones under the thicket. After this they felt motivated to travel on toward Ntshawini which was between Mvoti and Dukuza. When they had crossed the river, they were attacked by some weaklings of men who chased them for some distance. When they were nearing the small valley called Ngudwini, near Mvoti, where Manombe Zungu's sons and those of Mahlasela Ntuli lived, they saw big grass bundles and hid themselves inside them. When they were in the bundles, they rearranged the stalks so as to hide their tracks.

Soon after, the weaklings arrived and yelled: "Oh! We can see you! You are in those grass bundles. Hit them! There's the one who carries a witch's cat on his back. Oh, if I could get hold of you, bald one! What wouldn't I give!"

They stopped, looked at one another and started quarrelling over something that Makhwatha and Bantukabezwa could not hear. The two wanted to get out and run, but at that moment the child whom Makhwatha had carried on his shoulders began to cry. Makhwatha hastily covered her mouth. The sound startled the young criminals and they thought that it was coming from the valley which goes up the Ngudwini River. They turned and ran there, and indeed found a duiker with its calf drinking. They chased it, assuming that it was the calf they had heard crying, and forgot all about Makhwatha and Bantukabezwa. Because they were afraid, the two old men did not come out from their hiding place in the grass. It darkened, and when night fell, the moon returned. They saw it coming from the sea. It was red and round, like the rounded red-clay headgear used by married women. They saw it through the grass and kept quiet. From the hill on the other side they heard a bell ringing, but did not have any idea what it was for. They fell into a restless sleep after the child had been fed the remaining milk-gruel. Later, when Bantukabezwa sleepily crawled out of the grass bundles to run away, he realised that it was already morning, and quickly went back to wake Makhwatha.

In the clear morning light, they saw the village of the Kholwa, also known as oNonhlevu, meaning God-We-Are-Together, because the people living there had accepted Christianity as soon as the missionaries arrived. Makhwatha and his friend rose and shook out their sleeping skins, crossed the Mvoti and went up to the missionary, Mr. Grout, to ask for refuge there near the mission station.

They were given land north of Mvoti, and built a home there. At first the two of them lived in one hut. They were keeping an ear out for news of their wives. Then one day, they did receive news about them, and so the two men armed themselves and went to fetch them near Nyanganye, where some savages were holding them hostage, having robbed them of the little they had. They returned with their families. And so it was that the Makhwatha and Bantukabezwa homesteads remained on excellent terms.

The girl they had found in the bundle grew up. She wore clothes, but like her fathers who had found her, did not like the teachings of the believers. Makhwatha called this daughter Nomkhosi, Mother-of-Decree, because he had found her while running away from Dingane's decree announcing the death of the whole Ndlela clan at Ntumeni. Despite his age, Makhwatha did not have many children: the boy born from Mamthimkhulu was still very young, and the one born from Nombanjane was not mentally sound, so he was of little account. Therefore Nomkhosi herded Makhwatha's cattle.

The footpath to the veld passed by the school where the children of the mission station were learning. Nomkhosi always heard the bell ring and saw the pupils getting together and standing in a line. Then somebody would come and drill them; everybody would march and at one point, neatly turn without missing a step, as can be seen even today at Marabastad in Pretoria, where young men and women do the turn-around as the rhythm of the school song dictates. Nomkhosi would move with her cattle and stop near the school to observe all these things. Later she would reflect on it, sitting with her dog, Nkondlwane, and again as she herded the cattle into the valleys. After a while she began to like these strange wonders, and wanted to discuss them with her sister Nontula, Makhwatha's senior daughter. But Nontula hated education, and was against all the doings of the Kholwa, so Nomkhosi ended up keeping quiet about it, but dying inside. She tried to content herself by watching it all while sitting down near the ant-heaps with Nkondlwane, the dog. Sometimes she would say: "Look now, Nkondlwane. Other children are studying and we are here. But perhaps it is better to look at it from a distance and not be locked inside the building every day. It's good, though, when they do the turn-around outside; I like it."

It was as if Nkondlwane could understand. He would lie down and make a noise, rolling on the ground. He would bark softly, run away swiftly, and then later come back and stretch himself at Nomkhosi's feet. When the children returned to their classrooms in the building, Nomkhosi would get up and slowly lead her cattle to the veld at MaNdelu.

2

Mpande's ties with the Boers accelerated the destruction of many small nations in Zululand. The small ones, who were afraid of being swallowed by the powerful ones, stole away to uThungulu, where they went to work for the whites in Durban. Mpande could not even control his household, so how could he lead the nation? We know that his sons, Mbuyazi and Cetshwayo, were fighting openly in his very presence; they were now so divided that Mbuyazi's group called itself iziGqoza, the Rebels. Mbuyazi was praised thus:

> Sudden-appearer like witchweed,
> He is a loner like the sun,
> He walks stiffly like a bush-warbler
> Counting the ridges.
> The buffalo of a disorderly place,
> The elephant with a tuft of hair
> He is the axe that surpasses other axes,
> The sedge that is cut and germinates,
> Part of it is Phunga
> Part of it is Mageba.

The people of Cetshwayo called themselves the uSuthu. Before long, they fought at Ndondakusuka, and Mbuyazi was beaten. And again the small groups of Zulus had to disperse, and they went in large numbers to the white man's land, seeking liberty and to live in harmony. Here in the white man's land, they did not need to live with arms and the spilling of blood. People's lifestyles here had really changed. A man would roll up his sleeves, and take a hoe to go and dig in the fields; or take an axe and cut wooden sticks to build his hut. He would mix the mud and smear his hut. The women in the white man's land were liberated, because all they did was to look after the children, cook, weed the fields, and take care of the houses and yards. People began to engage in trade, and the value placed on cattle and goats as the basis of wealth was diminishing. There were others who were leaving their homes to go to Durban to work. They worked for clothes and money, because the whites had come with coins of silver and gold, and it was said that whoever had those coins had all the riches. With the money one could buy clothes, cattle, and pay a full lobola for a wife. Young men would come from afar in Zululand, walking on foot to Durban to work for money.

Those young men who were able to understand something of the other nations' languages earned a little more money than others. These children that Nomkhosi used to see at school were preparing for the time when they would go to work for money in the white man's land. All this Nomkhosi heard but did not understand.

As Nomkhosi and her dog herded the cattle, always past the school towards MaNdelu, she came across many young men and women from Nkobongo, before Mhlali, on their way to school. One of these students was a boy called Nsikana. He liked to have fun and was the leader of the group from Nkobongo. He used to pass Nomkhosi and then shouted this proverb to her: "As for me, girl, if only I could be that dog walking where you walk – by the name of those of Nkobongo!" He would say that and pass. The others would laugh and that was it.

After a while, Nomkhosi began to feel bad about this; she was not used to being laughed at by anybody, as she was always alone herding cattle. One day she said, "What have I done to you that you talk to me like that, every time I pass?" Nsikana did not respond. He passed her as always, continuing to say the same thing. The girl began to feel ashamed. Eventually, when his stubborn persistence had diminished, Nsikana saw her one day and stole away, unseen, from the group. He hid himself in the forest, waiting for Nomkhosi. When she finally walked past, Nsikana asked, "You want to know why I shout at you every day?"

Nomkhosi was startled; she had not seen him. Her dog became suspicious, barked and approached Nsikana. It was a quick-tempered dog, and Makhwatha had chosen it for just that reason: so that it could protect the girl from troublesome boys.

But Nsikana spoke: "I do not really have the answer for you, girl, because I do not even know who you are and from which family you come. These cattle belong to Makhwatha, there in the north of the Mvoti ford. But I will answer you when I have grown, when I no longer go to that building where you see children doing a turn-around. You must wait for me and my answer. Promise me that you will wait, 'No matter when'." Nsikana said these last words so forcefully that it seemed as if he was about to hit her.

Nomkhosi was scared, and out of fright she said: "Yes, I will wait for you and your answer, 'No matter when'."

In the olden days, girls were beaten; anything could be done to them with a stick and abusive words. It was only the tenacious ones who confronted the boys themselves, who were spared. When talking to these young women, the boys always made sure not to use bad language.

Nsikana left and ran to school because he was late. Nomkhosi was left behind, and she felt a sense of fear that was to stay with her forever. She started to see images of Nsikana in her mind; she could see him clearly, and he would appear in her dreams saying, "Here, girl, if only I could be that dog that walks where you walk – by the name of those of Nkobongo."

Nkondlwane, the dog, began to greet Nsikana himself, and the cattle of Makhwatha seemed to exude Nsikana's smell. The song of our forefathers speaks true:

"I am like this because of love, I am like this because of rejection."

Nomkhosi was confused and did not know who she was. She was like this because she was ignorant, and not living with more mature girls who could explain to her what was happening.

One day Nomkhosi was herding her father's cattle and came across the group from Nkobongo, but noticed that Nsikana was not present. This happened for a month; eventually she simply had to know what had happened to him. She called one of the younger girls aside and cautiously asked her, and so heard that Nsikana had gone with his elder brothers to work in Durban for money. The child did not know when Nsikana would come back, but she knew that it would be a long time before he returned. This deeply upset Nomkhosi, but still, she did not understand why; she was not related to this boy, and there was no promise between them. All she knew was that he had insulted her, always shouting at her as if she had eaten his family's boiled mealies, and now she was waiting for his reply. Then a feeling of anger came over her. She kept quiet for a moment, then said to the child, "You can go, girl."

After some time, the wife of the Mfundisi, the white missionary Minister Grout, saw Nomkhosi herding her father's cattle, and she immediately liked Nomkhosi's neatness and asked her name. Nomkhosi responded, pointing out to her the district across the

Mvoti where the homesteads of the amaMboza, Makhwatha and Bantubezwe were built. One day the missionary came to Makhwatha's homestead and asked whether Nomkhosi could come and stay at his home to look after his children. Makhwatha agreed because his sons were now old enough to herd the cattle.

Days were counted differently in the land of the white man. There were now days on which no work was to be done. These were called iSabatha or iSonto. The Kholwa counted from this day, iSonto. The next day, uMsombuluko, people began their work, and that was followed by uLwesibili, the Second One, Third One, Fourth One and Fifth One. On the sixth day, the Kholwa went to the river to wash their blouses. You would find the rocks snow-white with women's clothes. On this day they were all finished with their work, preparing to go to worship the following day. Those who wore loin-skins and skin-skirts were not allowed into the Lord's house; they had to hide their upper and lower bodies. Here in the church the Mfundisi, the minister, advised people while they sat with not even one among them moving or making a sound. They would sometimes pick up a song and sing. The people had learnt many hymns that were sung. As Nomkhosi lived with the minister, she learnt to read and write in isiZulu, and learnt the prayers and the hymns. And this song she loved the most:

Come, Holy Spirit
Come, enter into us
We are eager to have you –
Let us experience you again.
Refrain: Holy Spirit
    You enter into us
    We are eager to have you –
    Let us experience you again. (*Zulu Hymnal* No. 106)

When they took up this song, the old men wearing izinjivane and izinkonjane, swallow-tail coats, sang it at a high pitch, joined by the old women showing their wrinkled faces, their voices imitating the reeds in the water. But always, above all these voices, Nomkhosi's own voice soared with beauty; it was like the beauty of a bee nestling in flowers rustled by the northerly wind in summer. Some of the other lovely voices singing belonged to Mhuhulu, Guinea-Fowl-of-the-Broad-Bladed-Assegai, whose song would be taken over by Bhevule, son of Mhawule of Dlozi. Thanks to to her exquisite voice, this daughter of Makhwatha was wanted by all the men. They noticed her, and tried various tricks to win her heart, while the women always congratulated her after the service. The young men made plans to win her over, and argued about the ways that would capture her heart. Should they use love potions? Ukuphalaza? Or just rub themselves with charms and then go and greet her? No, since they were afraid of her, better that they smeared her seat in church with love potions, so that when she sat on a chair the potion would get into her and she would start to love that person. Some young men considered ambushing her on her way to fetch water. But they had thought and thought and decided that their love potions would not work on Nomkhosi because she ate fish. The oils of a fish would make all the charms just wriggle away and not enter her body. Yes, they would simply melt away and not affect anything.

In the minister's house lived a young man who assisted him by preaching in the far-flung areas of the mission. This young man was educated and confident, and the minister thought no young woman at Mvoti was truly suitable for him. Nomkhosi was by now quite well acquainted with this young man. His name was Thomas, son of Nogiyela. When Nomkhosi was going home to visit her family, it was Thomas who escorted her. Nomkhosi grew to love him like her own brother.

They were coming from the north of Mvoti one Sunday afternoon when Thomas said to Nomkhosi: "Look Nomkhosi, here are the birds of the wind, the white egrets. They always fly in twos when they go to catch grasshoppers. There they are, going back home to their nests. Doesn't that interest you?"

"Yes, it's true; nature is amazing. I've also been thinking and looking at the beauty of the world, wishing I could fly far, far, to places those birds can't reach. Do you think they can fly till they reach Durban?"

"That I don't know, Nomkhosi, but what strikes me the most is that they always fly in twos."

"It is not the egrets alone that travel in twos. At home I saw two lambs playing happily together. This does not amaze me."

"You know, we have been travelling together now for a long time, talking about light things, like young children. Today, I want us to speak like adults. Nomkhosi, there's something I've been wishing to tell you ever since we got to know each other, but somehow, I am scared."

Nomkhosi did not hear him, because she was thinking about the two birds that might fly until they reached Durban, the land she did not know at all, and perhaps see Nsikana at work. Perhaps they would talk like the birds of the folk tale song:

Tayi, Tayi,
What do we carry with our mouths?
We are carrying the child's sour milk,
Where are we taking it?
We are taking it to Tayi,
Tayi of Soncengeza.

Thoughts like these ran through her head, so that when she noticed Thomas was no longer speaking, she said: "I can't hear, the wind blocks my ears." Thomas realised that this child was not here with him, and the matter ended there.

One day Thomas found Nomkhosi looking after the minister's children and said: "It is indeed a good thing to have clean children like these that you are taking care of, Nomkhosi. Do you think that if you had your own you would treat them so well?"

Nomkhosi laughed, touched the hair of the white man's child and stroked it. She held the hair with care, then parted it, making a line from the forehead backwards.

"My child's hair would be parted like this, because I would also like my husband to wear his hair like this."

Thomas smiled because he thought the parting of hair was something done by white people only. A black person's hair could not be divided in two like that of a white person. He turned to her: "Hmn. You are a good speaker, daughter of Makhwatha. But as for wearing hair like this, it is just a dream, as far as I am concerned."

Thomas stood and watched her as she played with the children, as if she herself was one. He went away, carrying his hat in his hand.

3

Going from Mhlali to Durban took a day and a half. The way cut through the forests and the plains of Gqolweni. It was a people's footpath, and though there were now wagons travelling there, there were no built roads. It was dangerous for groups of people to travel together at Gqolweni because there were now criminals there. From Gqolweni you went to oHlawe, travelling below the hills of Mvoti, crossed uHlange, then went straight to the banks of the Mngeni River. Then you cut through the marshes until you reached the harbour where Durban was situated.

Nsikana worked for three years and one month, and then began to miss home. On Sundays he did not forget to go to the Lord's house built on the sands where today the big house of the American Board is situated. Nsikana was a good singer of Christian hymns, but he did not want to join the groups of Christians; he just went there and sang with other people. After some time he had sixteen pounds, the red ones. In Durban he was a cook for men who raced horses. They gave him all their old clothes. He carried their bags if they were going to the races in Pietermaritzburg, and he also transported their horses for them. They would tell him to dress well and be presentable. One of these young men, speaking to Nsikana in Fanakalo, told him: "Hey Nsikana, you dress well, my boy, you dress much better than when you came here."

This young man, who knew Nsikana very well, parted his hair for him, leaving a line across the top of his head. One day this man told Nsikana to look at himself in the mirror. Nsikana had never seen himself in a mirror before. When he glanced in the mirror he saw a tall young black man standing next to a white man. He recognised the white man as his boss, but then asked: "Nkosana, who is there with you?"

The white man said, "Look closely, Nsikana. The other one who is there is this very Nsikana. Look how handsome he is." Nsikana was astonished at the white people's tricks.

When he was on his own in Durban, Nsikana began parting his hair, combed it well, and went to look at himself in the mirror. He would talk to himself and smile, just like a hamerkop, that bird of the witches, which stares the whole day at its image in the pond, as if saying: "Hmn. I am a handsome young man among my family, but I only have these and those weaknesses." Saying this, the hamerkop would walk wearily on the rocks along the edge of the water. Nsikana, too, was taking stock of himself as a young man.

The young white men used to tell Nsikana and his friends stories that they had heard from their own fathers, who had heard them from other white people who were older. There was always this friendship between these black and white men, something we see disappearing these days. When we do see it, the circumstances are usually desperate, such as when a black man rescues a white man from drowning. Or when they are travelling in such a dangerous place that all they see is the shared humanity which is in their blood and their bones.

One night they all stayed up, talking outside, because it was too hot to sleep. Then the elder nkosana said that he found the stories of Luganda, the land of the lions, amazing because they dealt with the bravery of the people there. Sometimes a group of people would go out after a lion that was known to kill people and animals. About a hundred people would come together, among them young children, women and men. They beat their drums, they shouted, they flattened the long grass in their charge towards the lion in a formation like a pair of horns. But as soon as the lion heard the noise, he shot out of his den and found himself surrounded by people jumping up and down; then he was completely confused by all the movement, and went up and down himself, not knowing what he was doing. As he jumped and fell down, the people hit him with spears or knobkieries.

Then somebody else told about a lion that did not care for animal meat, but exclusively ate human meat. One day a man from Luganda agreed to escort some white men carrying guns, who were going to shoot the lion. He was made to lie on a bier which was then put on the lion's footpath so that it would smell and then attack him. That night the moon came out and was beautiful; the hunters saw the man from Luganda walking unconcernedly to lie on the bier on the edge of the forest. He went there and stretched himself, lying on the bier, this man, while the whites climbed the trees, the bird's domain, and waited at a distance.

This naked young man lay flat. The hunters waited; one of them fell asleep, but when he woke up the coast was still clear, with no trace of the lion. From the trees they could see the young man still lying in the distance on the bier. Then dawn broke, and in the bleary light they saw a cat-like shadow approaching stealthily, crawling forward, fixated. It approached slowly but threateningly, just like a cat ready to charge a wild cat. The white men all prepared their guns as they could see that this huge cat was unaware of anything else but the prey lying on the bier.

The big lion kept on moving, kept on moving, treacherously. At last the hunters aimed at its head and shot. The lion sprang up with a mighty roar, shaking the ground. Now the hunters all shot and the bullets sliced through his skin. Then the lion fell down as if he was grass being cut by a sickle.

But something alarmed Nsikana: "What did the man on the bier do?"

The white man answered in broken isiZulu: "He just woke, sat up and rubbed his eyes, having just come out of a deep sleep in which he had good dreams."

Since they were all young men, they loved to tell stories about their experiences as young men striving to display their bravery, so that they would be popular among girls and be loved by them. One young man said that it was quite easy to display great valour in the land of the Mashona because it was full of elephants. Three young men would hide themselves in order to attack an elephant bull. One of them would get underneath it and stab it in the neck, near the ear. The elephant would be startled, and try to get to him. Then the second one would stand next to the path and stab the elephant in the shoulder blade, and it would thunder with pain. The spear in the shoulder blade would cause the elephant to turn and crash after the second man, who would be running away. Then it was the third man's turn. He would run after the elephant until he reached it, and stab it in the other shoulder blade. Now the elephant would be totally confused, not knowing who the enemy was and where they were coming from.

By then Nsikana and others would be lying on their stomachs, spellbound. If the white man stopped for a while, trying to fill his pipe, they would say in unison: "Go on, nkosana, it's still fascinating. How did the elephant end?"

Then another one would chip in, "As for me, I want to know where the *maidens* are because when we Zulus perform the ukugiya dance, being praised for our bravery, they are standing there, watching, amazed. And as you perform, they respond on every side, and the one who loves you cries, and your mother weeps tears of sorrow!"

Sometimes when a man saw that his story had created interest, he would leave it there, unfinished, so that the men would come back the next day to sit with everybody, overlooking the harbour, where the water is silvery clear if the moon is bright. The workers would finish their work quickly, and meet at the same place to listen to news of black people from other parts of the world. Then the white man would hear: "Continue, nkosana, we want to hear. Continue."

When the elephant bull had been stabbed, it began hitting itself with its tufted tail, and its ears flapped vigorously up and down; it ran on its short legs, making a loud trumpeting sound until it fell down, digging into the ground with its trunk, roaring. Then it was attacked again and stabbed with spears.

When it was completely dead, it was amazing to see what hordes of men, women, and young girls streamed from every direction with containers, coming to cut whatever they could of the elephant's meat. But the heroes got the tusks, which are very valuable, and which were eventually sold to people from other countries who took them overseas. The young women courted by these young men would send well-crafted beadwork to the men whose advances they accepted; a young man who had received beadwork would wear it around his waist and neck, or else on his head to show off the fact that he had gained a girl's love. It was not uncommon to see a group of girls clapping their hands for a heroic young man while his mother and father were more concerned about getting some of the meat.

When the story was drawing to a close, the men took their fighting sticks to leave, but Nsikana suddenly asked one of them, "Nkosana, do you have a love?" The young white man laughed and threw the question back at Nsikana. Mbokazi's son responded by saying, "I don't know if I have or don't have a love any more; when I left home I told a tall young girl, a young woman, to wait for me and not accept any other suitor." The men burst out laughing.

His friend said, "Come on, Nsikana, do you really think there's a girl that you could leave in her adolescence, and who will wait for you all this time?" Ridiculous, yes, and everybody found that very funny. "I thought you had grown up, Nsikana, but you are still a boy." Those were the words of his friend.

They left separately. Nsikana went to his hut, and left his friend singing "About Nobuhle, the girl who causes the boys to go mad."

Nsikana listened. He felt embarrassed by the question he had answered, wondering why he had suddenly felt compelled to respond in that way. Now he was a laughing stock. He remained outside his hut and saw that his bosses were still sitting outside in the same chairs they had been sitting on, smoking long pipes that sent smoke rolling up to the clouds. They gazed at the sea over the range of hills that ended at the Bluff. They saw fireflies at the harbour, as bright as fires burning in the middle of a dark forest. All of this was bathed in moonlight.

Nsikana looked out at all of this, and suddenly missed the girl he used to see walking with her dog, taking her father's cattle to herd at MaNdelu. He began to feel inexplicably happy, imagining himself sitting next to this girl. Not next to the sea shore by the harbour or the hill range, but next to the water of uMvoti where the blue agapanthus lily grows in summer and winter. And where the hairy grass spreads out and is grazed by cows that produce rich milk. He thought about things like these until he felt sleepy; then he slept there outside his hut, not covered by any blanket, till morning.

Another thing the white bosses used to ask Nsikana and his colleagues was whether or not they would like to be white one day. This was very funny because it brought forth a number of ideas. Some would say yes, they would love to become white, but Nsikana and his friend would say they would rather die black, because, as Nsikana's friend put it, "As for you white people, you are like a white cloth that is easily dirtied, and it easily suffers in the cold."

"Also the colour white is not a respectful and dignified colour like ours is. Look at our women. They are fit, plump, and fill the road where they walk. And yours are weak, thin and don't even have hands fit for carrying a hoe." When he said this, the whites burst out laughing, as customs like lobola, imvulamlomo or mouth-opener, and other things like that came to mind.

They realised that Africans saw the role of women quite differently, while white people regarded women as special beings, fit only to take care of the house and not to be seen by the sun. So, what would such a woman have to do with a hoe? The whites even told them that in their land overseas there are black people, and some rub themselves with creams and whitening powders to make themselves white. Here Nsikana and his friends had to laugh: these people were fools! As for them, they only liked the way white people dressed, especially the women, who hid their bodies, which were revered and should not be shown to everybody. And these legs that the men wore, they protected them when they walked in thorny areas.

So the two groups whiled away their time, arguing about things concerning white people and those concerning black people, until the time for jokes ended and they began to discuss political matters between the Boers and the English.

There was very great conflict between the English and the Boers who had settled at Khangela. One day, Nsikana and his colleagues were surprised by the young men they worked for. Red with rage, these Englishmen went to take down the Boers' flag, destroyed it, and set up camp near Point Road. No one ate that day. The food went cold in the pots.

"Hawu! Do you see this, Nsikana? The insects didn't eat today. In our place I was ordered to clean and oil the guns," said a Zulu man acquainted with Nsikana. "This scares me. Even though I am not familiar with the conflict of the white people, I can see something bad is looming," he said, while drawing deep on some dagga, and listening to it as it crackled and emitted curls of smoke. "Our own whites here are not ones to miss their food, but today they are absent. Do you also see those traitors who deserted from Zululand, I mean those who live at Msizini? I see they, too, are sharpening their spears. In the morning I saw their spears sparkling as they'd put them on wooden sticks." He then tried to take another pull from his dagga, but was clearly not really used to it. He ran home to rekindle the fire.

That afternoon they saw hordes of horses brought in. And that night Nsikana's senior nkosana told him in Fanakalo what their plans were. "Look, Nsikana, we are going to attack the Boers at Khangela. I don't know if I will come back. If I don't come back, look after my brother. Take good care of him."

As the man said this, Nsikana felt overcome with dizziness, as if he was dreaming, not sure of what he had heard; but he agreed and said, "Yes, nkosi, I will look after the home until you come back."

The soldiers left, taking long strides on the sand and cutting through the trees at the spot where it has been dredged today for ships from many other nations that now stop in Durban. Then, unexpectedly, by whose mistake nobody knew, one gun fired. The Boers' spies were around and spotted the English soldiers. They warned their own army, which readied itself. The Boers had their own camp higher up, and since moonlight washed everywhere, they saw the English approaching. They fired the first shots, and the stomachs of the English began to churn. They were confused, their horses were frightened, and the soldiers scattered.

The place was not as beautiful as what you see today. A large part was just a muddy bog, with reeds and ponds. So as the English retreated, made to scatter by the bullets, they ran and stumbled in the bog, and many of them died there. Their cannons, which had been hauled by horses, and some expensive guns, were abandoned there.

In the middle of the night Nsikana was woken by the junior nkosana who arrived covered with mud, his hair dishevelled as if he was a madman. "Hawu, what is it boss? What happened? Why do you come alone? Where is your elder brother?" The young man burst out crying. Nsikana tried to catch him but he simply collapsed. Nsikana hurriedly took off his wet clothes, laid him down on his sleeping mat and covered him with many blankets. Right through the night, until the next morning, he mumbled incomprehensible things about his brother.

The Boers did not waste any time. They soon advanced and attacked the English in their camp at Point Road. The English spies were caught and taken to Pietermaritzburg as prisoners while the rest were under siege for a full month. Quite soon their food was depleted; they started to eat the food of the horses that had survived, and they killed and ate a number of small animals as well – animals such as cats and dogs. Eventually a council met and the members came up with a plan to report these events at eBhayi. There was no other option. One of the older black men said to the councillors, "Chiefs, when the sun has set, let me and one of my chiefs leave with a boat; we will cut through the night and sail along the Bhiyafu. We will haul two or three horses and they can swim behind the boat. When we reach the other side, I will walk, my knees are still easy, and my chief can ride."

The council was amazed by the black man's wise scheme. One of them, by the name of Dick King, stood up and said: "My fellow men and councillors, I volunteer to go in the company of this man, Ndongeni, who has shown us the bravery of his people, the Luthulis. I will go tomorrow night." And indeed, by sunset the following day, the hero Ndongeni was already squatting under the nhlalamagwababa, the tree-where-the-white-necked-ravens-perch, close to the tied up boat. He was on his haunches, holding his weapons. Two horses were heard approaching.

"Is that you, Ndongeni?"

"It is me, nkosana. Is it time?"

"Yes, it is."

When Dick and Ndongeni set off with the boat and horses, the English felt some relief, and they were even able to talk. But for quite some time now, something had caused Nsikana to feel homesick. Now, he could not hold back his feelings. It became his habit to tell the junior nkosana stories about Zulu customs, praising the kings and the brave warriors in the evenings for him, so that the nkosana would not feel the pangs of hunger so much. He would even declaim the traditional praises, izibongo, when some of the junior nkosana's friends came to visit. He would recite praises for someone like Zulu kaNogandaya:

Thunderbolt roared out of nowhere,
Where there are no mimosa trees and no acacias,
Thick grass that can't be entered,
Runner until he reaches large crowds.

He would continue until he finished. But when he recited the izibongo of the kings, they always reminded him of his home near Mvoti. On one occasion he was reciting the praises, but then suddenly fell down and began to cry; but then, as if inspired, he performed the ukugiya dance before disappearing to his room to sleep.

And then it happened. One day a gunshot was heard from the sea. When they looked, they saw two ships approaching. The sound of bugles gave hope to the desperate soldiers and they all rushed out, even those who were weakened by hunger. All watched the water elephants which swallow people with pots, food and all, entering the Durban harbour. It was their rescue.

After a month Nsikana asked permission from his boss to visit home to see his father and mother at Nkobongo. He was told to find another man to take his place while he was gone, and he found a boy from Mzinyathi in the Qadi area to cover for him.

Nsikana started to pack his things. He took this and that, and looked for ropes to tie his baggage. He also saved some money to buy food on the way, and tried to recall the way he had come several years earlier. He did not receive letters any more, and he realised that a lot had changed since he left home. However, there would be transport to his area as goods were delivered from Eshowe, Dukuza, and other places near the sea shore, on the route to Zululand.

He armed himself – this young man of Nkobongo – and left with some young men who were going to Maphumulo. They said, "Since we cannot reach our homes today, it's better to start our journey while the sun is warm." So Nsikana went with these men whom he did not really know, secretly hoping that as the way to Maphumulo cuts through Mhlali, they would part somewhere on the road.

The men who were travelling in front were tall and muscled, wearing black and white earrings made of thick bone. They were talking, and one of them said: "You know, my friend, I am going home empty-handed. I worked at Point Road for two years but there's no money to show for it."

"What? How can you do that, knowing you left a woman waiting at your home, and you have even started paying lobola for her?"

The other said, "I really don't know what I am going to say to my father. I drank brandy with all the money. I only have four pounds."

"That's bad news, man, very bad news."

They walked on, but then he started to talk again: "I've come up with a plan. How about we rob this thing we are travelling with?"

The other one kept quiet. "You know, this young man from our place, because he was working well. We can just cut his throat and throw him into the water, take the money and whatever we can, and leave."

The other one first said nothing, but later showed his colours: "No, brother, I do not agree. This boy was placed in my care by his father. He said I should protect him from harm. And secondly, he is my brother-in-law. When I see him, I see his sister, Ntombiyembuqa. No, my man, I don't agree. I would rather die in his stead."

They continued with the journey. Nsikana followed right behind with others, talking about Durban, the war, and work, not knowing what the two men in front were discussing.

"Who's this other boy, then, who we are travelling with?"

The companion answered: "He comes from Mhlali and is also going home. Since he trusts my brother-in-law, they are travelling together. I wonder how well *he* worked?"

And so they made a plan to pickpocket Nsikana and take all his belongings.

When the sun set, they had left Mdloti and were approaching the flat lands of Gqolweni, which is truly alive with thugs, criminals and bullies. They left the road for each to find a place to sleep, pointing their fighting sticks to where the sun set, as was the custom with all travellers. This was done so that people would not get lost when they woke up, and could leave bad luck behind, only following the good luck ahead.

The ancestors of an antelope could also warn if danger was close at hand: Nsikana sensed that something terrible was about to happen to him. All along their journey that day, he feared the eyes of the two men who were walking ahead of them. His body felt uneasy when he lay down to sleep. Therefore he carefully bided his time and then simply disappeared, as if heading to the outhouse. He took all his money with him and buried it under some dung near an ant-heap, and returned to his spot for an uneasy sleep. If he had known the area better, and if it had not been notoriously filled with thugs, he would have run away from those men. It was by now quite dark. The darkness was weakened only by the stars and the marsh grass that was always watching. Far away, near the homes where he had seen flickers of fire, he heard the nightjar calling, "Zavolo, zavolo, milk for your children." It felt good to be back in the wild, having not been a sleeper-in-the-wild for a long time. He stayed awake, looking up and listening to the nightjar until he fell into a deep sleep.

No sooner had he fallen asleep than he was awoken by a man who hit him with a stick, saying, "This thing sleeps so deep that he is clearly born of dirty people. Wake up and tell us what work you did in Durban. We force a man to pay, especially if he hopes to be protected by us." He said this and hit him again with his stick. Nsikana kept quiet, and his eyes started to water as he realised that he had been betrayed by the people he was supposed to trust.

"Hawu, people, are you now going to cut my throat here in the wild, even though we were travelling together?"

The man grabbed him by the neck and said, "Shut up! Shut up! Who are you talking to like that? You don't even know me, so don't dare talk of trust!" He struck again, and this time hit Nsikana's knee. Nsikana fell down. For a moment he thought about fighting back.

"Oh, sorry! You of the central house, have mercy my lords. Search my things, and if you find any money, it's all yours. But the truth is I lost all my money when the English were fighting with the Boers at Khangela. I go back home empty-handed."

They searched and searched and found nothing, then went back to him, "Listen here, you boy, we know you've hidden the money. We will beat you until all you have left is your tongue." And then they started to beat him viciously. They beat him and left him there and took all the little things he was hoping to give to his mother at home and the things given to him by his bosses. They took everything and left only what had no value at all. They left him in the cold of Dotsheni and in the water-myrtles of Gqolweni. They meant him to succumb to the weather and die there.

4

It was on a Sunday morning that Nomkhosi asked the minister's wife for permission to go and preach in the church near Sihlahleni. The way to that church cut through the flat plain at Mandelu, which was the same way that went to Durban. As Nomkhosi was walking on this path, she reflected on how times had changed. Here she was, travelling this same path of old, but as a grown young woman holding her Bible and hymnal. Three years back, she had been nothing as she walked this road, herding her father's cattle. She walked until she reached a spot where she used to sit with her dog, Nkondlwane, to watch the school children do the turn-around.

She remembered the group from Nkobongo and that boy who used to shout at her. She even remembered his name: Nsikana. She laughed aloud when she got near the tree where Nsikana had said that he would not tell her why he shouted at her. She suddenly realised that she indeed had feelings for this boy. Why was it that she missed him so much, and why did she want him to give her that answer today? Why was it that he stuck so deep in her heart even though it had been years since they last saw each other? Yes. But perhaps there were other girls in Durban smarter than she, with whom Nsikana had fallen in love soon after his arrival. If not, why hadn't he come back? If he had come back, why hadn't he shown up at the church? "A boy forgets but a girl suffers alone in love," she said and continued her journey.

She structured the subject she was going to preach about while climbing the Place-of-a-Wild-Cat hill, Kwesempaka, a hill covered with tree euphorbias, until she saw her little "church". This Sunday the church service was led by the daughter of Bantukabezwa who had married into the Mdleyana family. To this day, the church is referred to as At-the-Tree, because there is still no building yet – there is not even a bell – but some people worked full out for the Lord because they remembered the words: "It is said that even under a tree, and even if there are only three people, the Almighty will be there with them." If you were at Mvoti, you would have seen a small donkey pulling a small wagon, coming from the home of Mr Grout in order to further Nomkhosi's work. It was sad to see so much work initially not being championed by anybody; good deeds coming to nothing, like wild flowers blooming when they are still low, and drying out, their beauty dying there in the wild. If the preaching of the word had succeeded here at Sihlahleni, today there would be bells ringing at a huge temple of temples.

Nomkhosi walked alone until she reached the church. She held the service and completed it, then stayed to teach those who wanted to join the church. When she had finished, women came to her and surrounded her, thanking her for the lovely and inspiring service. They all walked together until they reached the way to Durban, where they left her. Next to the road, Nomkhosi stopped and gazed to the south. Far away, she could see smoke rising, and, with difficulty, could make out Mhlali and Nkobongo where the sons of Phephethwayo and Malamba live today. Her mind was still occupied with Nsikana, wondering whether, during these three years, he had remembered the girl he left herding cattle. At that moment she felt someone touching her shoulder and taking her books. It was Thomas, son of Nogiyela. Thomas had heard that Nomkhosi was at Sihlahleni and decided to make use of the opportunity.

"What is it, Nomkhosi, what is the place that you miss?"

Nomkhosi first kept quiet, then said, "As I was walking I was remembering how, when I was young, I herded my father's cattle like a boy. Leading them to fields, I used to come across boys who were studying in the white school building. I just cannot rid my mind of those boys."

"But why do you care about *those* boys, because they belong to the heathens and you are a Kholwa?" Nogiyela's son asked. He saw himself as the only one who was worthy of Nomkhosi; even more so today, because he was holding her Bible and hymnal for her.

"I know, but I was just remembering them because they used to make me laugh when I was alone with the cattle. I wish I could meet them again to see if they speak better English than I now can, because they used to look at me as though I was just a stupid person."

"All right. Then it doesn't matter. I was beginning to be concerned."

They continued their walk in silence.

"Ah, but now I suddenly remember something, nkosazana, my lady. I heard people talking about a young man from Mhlali who used to flirt with you. That quite hurt my feelings, and you have to realise, nkosazana, that it would hurt me terribly if there was a man in this world whom you could look at with eyes filled with more love and pain than when you look at me. I want to tell you what's in my mind about you, but my words disappear in the darkness of my mouth, just as soap disappears in the hands of the washer."

But it was as if Nomkhosi did not hear; she ignored him and started to hum a song. Later she said: "I hear," but continued humming, not responding to Thomas's words. "I remember very well that one of those boys went to Durban."

"Oh, are you ignoring me because you are holding on to this boy from Mhlali who went to Durban? Is that what is happening?" Thomas sounded very angry.

"No. It's not true."

"How do you know that Nsikana was not taken by the whores who are beginning to fill the towns, pretending to work but actually luring those who really work?"

Nomkhosi said: "You are mistaken, Qwabe."

"No, I am not mistaken; I know these stories. When they reach Durban, people become lone bulls, nobody even knowing the holes they sleep in; they are always up and down on the roads. Do you really think that you, filled with the spirit and humility of the minister's place, can compete with the "finches of Durban" who fly in the air, wearing shoes? Even that boy, whatever his name, is enjoying long-legged and light-skinned ladies. You lie to yourself if you think you can compete with things like that."

"No, he's not like that, you're so wrong."

"You will ask me and peel my tongue – and in future see I am right! He won't even have a black valueless ndibilishi coin when he returns."

"Well, we don't know that. If he doesn't bring it, it will mean something happened; bad luck befell him."

This absolutely infuriated Thomas. He could not help remembering that in the past, when a girl responded in such a cheeky way, the boy would run at her with a stick and there would be chaos until she was rescued by her brothers. Now this only still happened in Zululand. He realised that the best way to attract her to him was by telling her about a conversation that he had heard the minister have with his wife after they had received a letter in the post: "Here's another story, nkosazana. Let's not quarrel over nothing. In Durban something very bad happened. The white people had a ferocious fight; they dragged one another into the mud, and multitudes of the English soldiers were killed by the Boers. They say all the people from Zululand – large numbers of them – died for their employers; not even one remained."

"Awu? That is terrible! You heard the minister talk about it? I feel sorry for them."

"The letter also said that even though some men survived, they are under siege. They get killed every day. The ancestors are angry; they are punishing them for all the filth that is in Durban. It is best that we stay in good company and accept what is destined for us, because the way I see it, and whichever way I look at it, I see you destined to be mine and I destined to be yours. Or else, why did the Lord bring us together here at the minister's home, to be the only ones who spread the work of God while others are still languishing in darkness?"

These words found their way to Nomkhosi's heart, and she gradually began to think differently. Indeed, even if she did love Nsikana, had he ever approached her? Because what he did – shouting at her – was what every boy did to annoy a girl who was a stranger. And who knew whether Nsikana had been taken by those finches from Durban? And even if they had not taken him, who knew if he was still alive? If white people were dying, how much greater the risks were for a person like Nsikana! All these things ran through Nomkhosi's mind, and she was surprised to hear herself say, "What brought us together at the minister's is indeed amazing."

Thomas did not know that if you want to win over a woman, especially if she has fallen for another young man, you should start by praising that young man, and recount all the heroic things he has done, while you humble yourself and become someone to be pitied. In Zululand, a man would never go to a woman saying, "Come on, nkosazana! Who do you think you are to reject me? Are there *any* worthwhile girls at your home? Are your sisters also

49

skinny-legged just like you? Do you think you *deserve* a man like me?" That young man could then jump this way and that way, but the girl would laugh a pretended laugh, then burst into tears because he had insulted her and her household. The young man would have to disappear quickly before he was caught.

It would be much better if he found out when she was fetching water, then he could come and block her way, and teasingly ask, "My sister, are you swallowing my words along with your family's boiled mealies?" He would tease and joke a bit and then leave her. She, too, would play up to it so that the young man could see she was enjoying the teasing aimed especially at her. Then he would relent and take more notice of her.

In the white man's land, all the traditional flirting and courtship changed into something very different. If you teased a young woman about some shortcoming, she would go straight to the mirror, see her own beauty, and then come to you as she was yesterday. "No conman can lick his own back!" the elders said, so she would reject the young man, believing that he was insulting and undermining her. Thomas lacked the wisdom of the old people, but he had other advantages; nevertheless, a girl's heart could change like the wheel of a wagon. The two of them strolled along towards home, talking about religious matters, and putting the issue of love on the back-burner.

The minister thought that when these two protégées of his got married, they would expand the work he had started within the black nation. He loved them both, and thought that, in the future, when the land was divided into reserves, he would be sure to give them a piece of land here at Mvoti, which would be a reminder to their children of their history here. He always had this dream, but it was never fulfilled, never realised by him, this minister of the believers. It is, indeed, often like that: those who wish to see the fruits of their dreams find that it will be others who will harvest those dreams for them when they have passed away. Or they find that the fruits take a long time to ripen. It is normal, even nowadays, that a person's thoughts and wishes can create barriers like wide rivers, for they cannot know how the water from those rivers will flow. Perhaps those barriers are like rivers flowing through a treeless earth, so that when hot and strong winds come, all the dust blows into the rivers, and the rivers are clogged and covered up before they can ever be seen as we imagined them in our dreams.

The minister shared his thought with Thomas, and he, for his part, was happy to realise that the minister loved him this much. He started to take lessons on how to preach, and it became clear that his relationship with Nomkhosi was ripening. It was decided that when they got married, a huge Christian feast would be held for them. Nomkhosi began to watch Christian weddings and compared them with traditional Zulu ones.

In the traditional Zulu wedding, the bride would come out with her group, carrying a cow's tail with its thick tassel of hair, and a short spear that she would use to dance with to show that her virginity was no more; she would carry this short spear until the end of the wedding. On her head, she hung the gall bladder of the cow that her father had slaughtered for her before she left home for her new home. This gall bladder symbolised the relationship between the two families involved in the wedding; the bride would take the gall bladder to her new hut and place it at the sacred spot called umsamo. The young women and girls who accompanied the bride would dance from the evening, when they arrived, until sunrise the following day.

Instead of going to a church, the bride's group would go to the veld early in the morning to a spot they called esihlahleni where they were given a goat or a cow to cook there in the veld, and all the relatives who came also brought food. During this period, the marriage negotiator was like the minister in a church, because he had to control the time and fetch the bride's party to the dance area. And indeed, the bridal party would arrive in unison and form two lines in the dancing area, which had been swept by the women using the tails of various wild animals. They were praising the girl they had been living with as a little scoundrel and a nobody. On that day both families teased the other: those of the bride joked about bad things concerning the groom, while the groom's family recounted all the bad things they could think of about the bride and her family.

During those weddings, the bride had her own assistant who supported her, standing opposite her when the dancing lines were formed. They would start a song together, hiding their faces, the bride always pointing her short spear down, and her assistant pointing her short stick down. The other girls and young women would take up the song, also looking down, and sing until the song reached the right pitch, then the dancing would commence.

The bride and her assistant would start to dance in an open spot. The bride would come out and dance towards the groom's side. After dancing her way back, two other girls would dance forward and also perform in such a way that the groom's family would say, "Hey, she is a dancer and so-and-so's daughter; who is this? Unbelievable!" So some men would say, "Grow old, body; stay well, my heart. No tree ages with its bark." If the bride's group was dancing, the men would not join in, but stand together and quietly take part in the singing.

When the bride's group had finished the dance, the father of the bride would begin a speech which, in effect, meant that he was presenting his daughter to her new family. He would offer thanks to his own kings and his grandfathers, until he began to praise his daughter as if she was a well-known maiden. The young men, adept performers, would come forward and start the ukugiya dance in appreciation of the bride's father's words. Women from every side would ululate. During this time one could often see wet eyes and tears falling as many people remembered their ancestors. If the main performer was a warrior who had killed in battle, his family would pick up sand and hurl it at him when he had finished dancing, praise him and say: "You go, so-and-so, you, who did such-and-such!" The man would return to the dance area, shaking his head like a bull that had just destroyed an ant-heap, and making threatening movements. The women, for their part, would continue to compete in the traditional dignified walk, ukugqiza, praising him for the things he had done, and appreciating the words that had been said, and the dancing of the young men. There were women who excelled at ukugqiza, and who were well known for it, like KaMabuza of Ngcobo who married Mhlakaza son of Nkonzo of Ngwane at Mvoti. Even today, this dignified walk is popular at weddings, including those of the educated. At Mvoti, it is still widely performed.

When these activities were finished, the groom's father would begin to speak for his son, and the groom's group would retire to dress up because soon they would take over the stage. At this point other visitors who were not part of either party had to perform, because it was a bad thing to leave the stage empty – that might bring bad luck.

The groom's party would approach, following a cow or bull, marching together, and singing their own song. The bull or cow would low and the young men would dance until they fell to the ground. It is true that there was something that tied a man to a cow and joined them together on the earth where he was born, even if the times and laws changed. That is the truth. The young men would follow the old men, who were leading, and the women came last. Now it was the men who did their dancing for the bride's group and the women only provided support. The groom's party, with their shields and sticks, danced isigekle, in which the young men stood still, only allowing their torsos, heads and hands to move, with the wrists so agile that it seemed as if the hands had no bones, pointing the sticks left, right, forwards and upwards. Whoever outperformed other performers would be cheered by all.

After this everybody would disperse and prepare for the following day's slaughtering, because the current day's focus was on drinking beer. Nomkhosi had known weddings like this, but when Christianity arrived, things changed: this was because Minister Grout had sometimes visited to watch the dancing, and seen how young men performed the ukugiya until they fell into a fit of madness caused by having killed a person, and how women ululated, walking jauntily like calves in the veld during the isigekle dance.

Actually, some things were really very scary. Once the minister saw Mhuhulu of Ngwane chase another man in a fit of madness. The victim ran and hid himself under the minister's bed, but Mhuhulu followed him, hot-blooded and crazy, and entered the minister's house, his room, and then stabbed the person under the minister's bed. This the minister never forgot, and he often talked about it, even to Nomkhosi. As more and more people were joining the church, they learnt that the laws there were different from those of the people outside, and their weddings were performed differently. The minister prohibited ululating and the making of beer to get people drunk. The ukugiya dance was also prohibited within the mission. The wedding songs had changed, and were separated into two types. On the day the bridal party arrived, there was the same dancing and dignified walks as in traditional weddings. They would dance the umqhuqhumbelo, which was similar to isigekle, except that it used feet for its attraction. The competition would go on till morning. The following day they would go to the church to formalise the marriage in front of the church community. They would sing church songs, and then sing others for entertainment after the church marriage ceremony.

Even though people appeared to accept it all, it was hard that the minister refused even things like ululating. They always fumed quietly inside when there was a wedding, until one day, after leaving the church, Nxaba's wife burst out in ululation because the young men and women had their legs twisted as they did the tamba dance.

"Well, it doesn't matter now," she laughed. "There are many cows in the kraals, and the minister can take one as a fine if he so wishes. Kikiki! Is there not a girl who is going away? Why do we then walk as if someone has died, as if our mouths are tied?" As soon as she said that all the women started ululating with voices that for too long had been imprisoned. Yes, their voices sounded like water breaking the wall that had hemmed them in. The women ululated and shouted until their voices echoed in the hills and valleys of Mvoti. One woman said, "Kikiki, all is well at home! There's great beer. The girl, the young woman, is going away. So say we of the old homestead; we of the big homestead, we of the school of Mvoti which has gaps in the teeth, which is green-haired, being combed by maize cobs."

Then again the women broke into ululation. Nxaba's wife could not contain herself when she saw what a good dancer her son was. Even the air could not be quiet when he leapt and performed astounding movements so fast and rhythmically while the concertina was held high by the son of Mbambo, Mafushane. No. It could not be. Her son, Jacobus, light-skinned and bewhiskered, was well known among the young men, and when his mother dared to ululate, she was not daring for nothing, but remembering her forefathers who were no more.

Nomkhosi attended this particular wedding and was shocked to see people disrespecting the minister, breaking his law, ululating like outsiders. At the same time, she had a feeling of being light-headed and drifting away, thinking that she too would ululate if young people performed like this, because what could be wrong if women ululate in celebration? However, the minister had made the law and these women were breaking it. Nomkhosi ended up saying they were wrong, even though she herself could not see anything wrong.

The old women walked as if they were going to pounce on someone when their mouths opened. Nomkhosi saw all this and said nothing. However, this was the beginning: people were growing wings, realising that some things were forbidden while there was nothing bad in them. From that day, ululating became the norm, and we never heard that the minister ever fetched a cow from Mdleyana's homestead as a fine for the breaking of the law by his wife, Mseyiseyi. The ways of celebrating expanded when the young men, coming from Durban, brought concertinas. When they played, young men would leap into the air, saying they itched from matekanyane, sand fleas; so said Makhabeni's son, Msindo, and Hlonono's son, Langeni, and that of Mbambo, Mmbiyana, who was not shy to speak his mind.

Marriages were plentiful, and all the young women wanted weddings in which they would walk gracefully with their white umbrellas in their hands, and be grouped together with their friends in the tamba dance, and be led by a concertina player known as maskandi. Those outside the school were also attracted to this type of wedding. They would come carrying fighting sticks, and stand and watch the young men and women of the Kholwa playing with this mfungumfu, the concertina, which caused the hair to tingle when it was played, and the whistles would play as if there was witchcraft in all of it; charms that move emotions. People would sell their cattle to buy the concertina, which played until young women wailed and ran to the mountains. "Oh, how foolish we have been, the clever ones have exploited us."

Nomkhosi used to laugh when she saw the things that people returning from Durban brought with them, and that caused them to change their ways. Indeed, people had changed, and nothing could stop them. The sun had risen from below, and everybody took their hoes and ran against time so that darkness did not catch up with them.

Nomkhosi again had this feeling of something drifting away within her, telling her inwardly that the boy who had left and said he must be waited for, would return and change her, making her something else. And for a while she forgot about the minister, who was far away in his house, and she forgot about Thomas, who had found his way into her heart. It felt good to walk with this group, being one of them, and to do the tamba dance with the other young women. It was good to talk about the Durban she did not know. Where waters are crossed by ships that swallow people and spit them out on the other side, and when they come home they are carrying concertinas, head-kerchiefs made of silk, red shoes, and umbrellas. It thrilled her to be in the midst of these people. Yes, indeed, it was good.

5

When the Boers had been forced to retreat from the Durban lagoon, they went to Pietermaritzburg, where their government presided. Some, disillusioned, said they could no longer stay in Natal: in the south they were goaded by Faku's Mpondo; in the east they were jabbed by the English, and in the north the Zulus closed one eye to them and said, "Mpangampongo, you sleep and the spear stabs you." They packed their things, crossed the escarpment and disappeared. Only their small dirt remained.

In Zululand the sun had risen from the east. There were now a number of white missionaries who claimed to be teaching black people to believe in the Lord. They were not entirely removed from their fellow brothers and sisters overseas and those in Durban, who kept in contact with one another through writing letters. These would arrive in Durban to be transported by horse-wagon for distribution all around Zululand. At Dukuza there was a horse-wagon station that sent wagons weekly to oHlawe and from there to Durban. They were driven by trusted people because they carried the ministers' luggage, brimming with clothes and books.

One of these wagons that had come from Dukuza passed through Gqolweni early one morning, cutting through the forest-myrtles where the criminals from Maphumulo had beaten Nsikana.

After the attack, Nsikana had fainted and was unconscious for the rest of the night, not knowing where he was, his mind numb and deeply disturbed by dreams that came to him while he thought he was dead. During the night, an icy wind blew and woke him, but he had no idea where he was. An attempt to move yielded no result; his body was heavy and felt as though it were somebody else's. The cold filled the valley; it was now the middle of the night, and dawn still far off. He was so stiff from the cold that he could neither talk nor move. As the ministers' wagon drove on its way to Durban, the drivers saw a human being on the side of the road, lying dead stiff like a piece of dry wood. They stopped the horses, and when they tried to talk to him, found that he was completely numb, not even able to whisper. Turning him over, they found his head and body riddled with wounds. Seeing these wounds, they assumed that it was someone from the mission who had been attacked by criminals who had robbed him of whatever he had. They felt very sorry for him, covered him with blankets, and put him on their wagon heading to Durban – all without Nsikana realising it.

They left him where they dropped their loads. They took what they had been sent for, changed horses, and returned early the next morning. When they reached home they talked about this in the kitchen where all the workers sat, and where Nomkhosi was preparing food for them.

"Oh, they really damaged a young man with sticks, men! We felt sorry for him and took him in our wagon and left him in Durban."

"Who are those terrible people?"

"We don't know. We were in a hurry to get to Durban," said one man. "Just as we turned in the hills near Gqolweni, we saw this man lying next to the road. A full-bodied man, dark, and his state of dress and body suggest he's a Qwabe."

Thomas, who was also listening, responded: "You must be careful. It's dangerous these days to pick people up who are sleeping near the roads, or doing whatever they may be doing."

"Awu! What are you saying, Nduna? We must leave him even if we can see that he is severely wounded and attacked?"

"Yes, it's dangerous! How can you tell? Perhaps you are the ones who attacked him and tried to rob him. Durban is the white men's land and subject to their laws."

"Is that really so, Nduna?"

"Yes, I know these things."

Nomkhosi, who had asked that question, laughed and then left the men because she had finished serving food to the workers. After that conversation, however, the men never again gave a lift to anybody whom they saw was in need of help. Returning to Durban, they felt a bit shaken, nervous that they might be caught and accused of being criminals who had almost murdered a man.

On the day they left him in Durban, Nsikana was taken to a certain house which he recognised because his bosses used to send him there.

"Am I dreaming, or am I dead? You who are here, do you say I am still alive?" He said this and touched his head. Instead of finding his hair, he found white bandages covering his whole head, and when he pressed softly he felt pain. When he tried to turn where he was lying on a sleeping mat on grass that provided some form of mattress, he felt the stabbing pain all over his body. He was swollen and numb, and then asked again: "Am I dreaming or am I really alive?"

The people told him how he had been brought there by the wagon people who had picked him up at Gqolweni because they saw he had many wounds on his head. When he was left alone, Nsikana started to follow in his mind the journey with the people from Maphumulo. He followed it until the forest-myrtles where he had stashed his money next to the ant-heap. After that he remembered the beating, but he could not see what had happened afterwards. Now he saw himself in this house and thanked his ancestors that he had been saved. He asked to go to his boss, who was shocked to see him in such a bad state. He sought medicines for Nsikana, made of oils from otters, whales and other sea creatures, and other medicinal potions that the people of today usually see in the chemists of the white doctors. Yes, among the whites there are inyangas who are very clever, who have charms far more potent than those of Motlomi, Moshoeshoe's grandfather, and more potent than those with which Mbopha had strengthened Shaka to command respect. These white inyangas put some equipment on a person's chest and then say, "ncincinci", and then put it on his side, and they see what the sickness is with the eyes of their ears, because as they do this, there are some connectors that get put into the ears. Then they trap this illness with the ancestral spirits of the sea and it disappears. This happened to Nsikana too, and after a while he recovered.

Taking a letter from the white inyanga to the chemist's place, he collected his own medicines and there he met a young man who had just arrived from Mvoti. One day, some time later, this boy wanted to write home but he did not know how to write. Nsikana wrote for him, and also read to him the letters that were written back to the boy. One day this boy received a letter saying: "Thomas, Nogiyela's son, will be married according to the law of the believers to Nomkhosi, Makhwatha's daughter, who lives with the minister. But there is rumour that there is a man who proposed to her a while back, who left her and said he is going to work. But these are just stories, people always talk."

Nsikana tried to restrain himself but his heart revealed him. It said to him: "That is you, Nsikana, who told the girl to wait until you return, 'No matter when'. You will let her know what you think of her. To this day she has been waiting for you." Nsikana went back to where he lived, taking his medicines with him, and as he applied the ointments to his wounds, he sung sad songs about his deep desire to go home. We Zulus, whenever we think of something, wish for something, or miss it, if we are sad or happy, we set it down, we sing it in a tone that accords with our emotions at the time. This is what confuses other nations about the Zulus: because whether we are oppressed or free, it's the same, we vent it through song. Nsikana, too, hummed his own words; it was his way of dealing with the problem known to him and Nomkhosi alone.

On top of all his agonising about Nomkhosi, the realisation that he had lost all his money when the thugs from Maphumulo robbed him, made him despair. He also could not remember the place where he had hidden the money. He tried to recall it, but to no avail. All he remembered was that it was under a myrtle tree, near an ant-heap a few feet from the tree. The dung under which he had stashed the money must have dried out long ago and was probably covered by grass. All these things made him feel dejected, and he had many sleepless nights.

The next week he asked the boy from Mvoti when he was going home, because he wanted to travel with him. The way was not as remote as it had been previously, and wagons transporting goods were now more frequent on the road. But what really worried Nsikana was that he had to work to earn more money; indeed, why would he go back if he did not have any money? He would certainly be a laughing stock. And how would he pay the lobola for the girl whom he might cause to spill the beer that she had brewed with Nogiyela's son?

The boy had worked for two and a half months and was due to go home at the end of the month. They started to pack, preparing their weapons and food for the road. Since Nsikana knew everything about the way up to Gqolweni, he determined the time to leave. He suggested that they set off in the afternoon and travel until they reached a new white man's mission that had been established at Mvoti. His friend agreed. As they made their way, they met men coming from Zululand and asked: "How is it fellows, is there food back at home?"

"Oh, there's feasting back at uThungulu; we are on our way to see what is happening at home."

"So where can we sleep, brothers?" they asked, while the two young men were walking away.

The young men stopped, catching their words. "Oh, don't worry, there's a place not far away now; just pass that mountain and turn, cross a big river and at its mouth you'll see white houses."

"Thank you. It is clear that life is good at uThungulu. Your bodies and confident walk say it all. Even in Zululand, by Mpande's name, young men like you are no more." The men turned and walked on towards Durban.

By sundown Nsikana and his friend had passed Ohlange and crossed to the hills heading to the Mdloti River, its water visible below. Turning their eyes upwards, they saw a number of tents and makeshift houses erected there. As darkness was falling and it was dangerous to sleep in the open with so many wild animals roaming, they asked for a place to sleep. They were shown to a hut in which there was a fire and other people who were also waiting for the morning to start their journey. They were all heading for Durban, and had not been there before.

The talk in the hut was all about the war, and the fact that Cetshwayo was now effectively acting as the king, in his father, Mpande's, kingdom. Mpande's sons, Cetshwayo and Mbuyazi, had waged a war at Ndondakusuka, and Mbuyazi's army had been defeated, yet no one knew where his body lay. Some said that Mbuyazi had run away to Pietermaritzburg when he realised that his army, iziGqoza, was being eaten alive by the uSuthu. Others suggested that he had killed himself in a mysterious way, because he did not want his body to be touched by Cetshwayo or any member of the uSuthu.

This was discussed till dawn. Young men from Mdloti who were not working for the whites sang, giya-danced, stretched themselves out, and smoked dagga without any worries. Other young men who were employed by whites were smoking cigarettes in their own rooms and reading papers by candle-light. Nsikana watched all this and meditated about the different attitudes of the people from Zululand, who were still doing things in traditional ways, and those who were used to the whites' way of life; he tried to imagine what it would be like for their sons one day if they ever had any.

Nsikana felt that he was not part of any of this. His mind was engrossed by the girl he had last seen three years and some months earlier, wondering how old she was today and what kind of person Thomas was, and, especially, how big and strong a young man he was. But no matter how big he was – he could be as big as two mountains put together, for all he cared – Nsikana knew that things would change if only he could have eye contact with Nomkhosi and remind her of her old promise to wait for him, "No matter when!" And just when the fire was really warm, the men from Zululand talking happily with their luggage along the wall, a dark cloud fell on him, a cloud about the money he had lost near Gqolweni. Even if Nomkhosi accepted him, he would have no money to lobola her. All his other thoughts faded away, and grimacing and clenching his teeth, he went outside, leaving his friend to watch over his luggage.

Then, deep in the night, they fell asleep and there was utter silence. However, those Zulu men not used to deep sleep would often wake up and talk: "I wonder where I – my father's son – will be sleeping tomorrow." And then the other who was also awake said: "It's as if you are talking about me; my heart is at home. I can imagine my wives, MaShandu and MaBhulose, staying awake in the war-torn land." Then they would be quiet again, and the frogs could be heard croaking down in the river, announcing summer, and then also keeping quiet. Someone would snore and then talk in his sleep. In the centre of the hut, the fire had burned to embers, about to die out, a crust of ashes covering the coals, with the people inside not able to see each other. Finally Nsikana, too, fell asleep, to be woken by a cock crowing. The morning star had risen from below. Nsikana woke his friend. They said goodbye to the others and set out for the waters of uMvoti. By sunrise they had climbed Nyaninga, passed oHlawe (today known as oThongathi) to walk through the plains of Gqolweni. As it got hot, they were nearing the myrtle trees. They sat under the trees and talked: "This is good. We have travelled well because it is not yet afternoon; by sunset we will be parting ways, as I'll be entering my home area."

"Yes, my brother, we have travelled; let's sit down and open our vessels and drink. This spring water looks good."

"Indeed," said Nsikana.

They sat under the myrtle tree and drank sugared water, and ate bread and meat. Then Nsikana said, "I am going to look around." As they were eating, Nsikana had been studying their surroundings, thinking, "We slept there, I went this way to hide the money." He went to the place he had identified but was still unsure about the exact ant-heap as he now saw two close together. He searched the area, digging here and there until he found where the money should be. He dug with the handle part of his stick. Then, unexpectedly, he heard a clanking sound. And out came the money. He picked it up, his eyes blurred by fear, and his hands shaking as though someone was watching him. He counted it and everything was still there! He fell on his knees and thanked the Lord, and ended by summoning the spirits of his ancestors. His white bosses liked him a lot and the younger one who had survived the Boers had given him six pounds, pitying him for his loss. All in all, now he now had twenty-one pounds.

Having covered the money in a large kerchief and fastened it tightly to his waist so that it would not make a noise when people passed by, he went back to the young man of Nkobongo, apologising for taking so long. But his friend was lying in the grass, tired by the journey and the sun. He woke him up, and they took their luggage and resumed their journey. Now Nsikana was telling stories. Their legs were stiff but his heart was light. Towards sunset they arrived at Mhlali, and Nsikana thanked his friend, the son of Man-made-Thunder-and-Lightning of Khuzwayo. They pointed out their homes to one another, and agreed where to meet on the following Sunday.

As soon as they had parted, Nsikana stood still, powerless, feeling as though he had not actually arrived home, but was dreaming. He smiled, and then, suddenly feeling fearful, he touched his stomach and realised that he was not dreaming. He picked up his luggage, took a turn at the road leading east and soon caught sight of his family's abandoned buildings. He passed the uninhabited buildings and headed for the current homestead. He smelt the fire made of mthombothi and mimosa trees, which his mother liked so much. He followed the shrubs making up the outer fencing of the homestead, avoiding entering through the gate because people would see him and delay him with useless questions until he disclosed his name. He went up to the upper part of the homestead where the gates of the girls and young women are, and the gate of the left-hand wife. He headed for the home of the second senior wife, his mother, and went on tiptoe to the wall of the hut. Here he stowed away his luggage in the vestibule, using the wood placed there to hide it, and then withdrew.

He went out through his mother's gate and hid near the fencing. He was so happy that he felt as if he was dreaming. He heard his mother's voice calling his sister, Nokuthela, who was now very tall. Way back when they were together performing the tamba dance, his father would praise her, saying, "long-necked she-goat, Magangane's butterfly that's never caught." She was beautiful, this girl, and the talk of the community. Nsikana heard the cows lowing in his father's kraal and their calves responding; he also heard those of his mother's house crying for their mothers. At the gate near the kennel, the dogs were barking at a person, and others told them to be quiet. He heard one of the goatherds who was late, but singing and whistling:

I lament my thing, Lizweni,
That which you left in Durban,
Oh my mother.

Then he would be quiet, and the voices of the lambs were heard near the tree, and their mothers responding with, "me-e-eh". Then they were quiet and the herdboy would start all over again, following his herd, his thoughts not maddened by the difficulties of the world. All this entered into the deep crevices of Nsikana's heart and created in him mixed feelings of sadness, tearfulness and a profound happiness.

Then the boy passed with his goats and sheep bumping each other and bleating, parting them and singing about his thing he left in Durban. Nsikana heard him until he disappeared into the valley still singing his song, not caring about the world. Nsikana wished he was this boy who did not know the world, who saw it as a folk tale.

6

Nsikana's family was made up of believers and heathens, the outsiders. They had a beautiful big homestead, built on the hill facing Mhlali and the sea where Phephethwayo's sons live. The land was covered with forests and palm trees, and the incema, the rush-grass that grows in depressions between the dunes, was tall and used to make sitting mats, eating mats and beer strainers. It was a landscape breathtakingly beautiful.

In the very week that Nsikana was to arrive, his mother's left eye began to twitch, and she would say: "Mamo, MaQwabe, my eye is twitching, I wonder who this familiar person is that I am going to see?" One day she was brewing African beer, and the sorghum-porridge swelled and overflowed from under the pot lid. If the beer does that, the elders say, it means it will be drunk by an outsider. Nsikana's mother just laughed and said, "I wonder, because Nsikana, whom I might say was the one to drink this beer, left me and went to Durban for good, leaving me 'oozing water like the meat of a dead animal'. Giving birth is like 'a problem-solver who brings hate unto himself'. Did I know that when I got old I would not even have a blanket to sleep on, unlike MaNkonzo and NoMaNyathela, who cover themselves with isisholo blankets and shawls, to show that they are the real mistresses of their homesteads?"

She lamented till dawn on the day Nsikana was to arrive. That same morning the cock stood in front of the door in Nsikana's mother's hut and crowed. They chased it away, saying, "It wants to boil in water." It crowed again, and they started to suspect something was about to happen. At sunset, they saw the mylabris blister beetle with its black and white colours, killed it, and burned it in the fire. The suspicions among those of Nsikana's house strengthened.

When it was fully dark, and the boys had separated the calves from their mothers and led them to the calves' corner in the hut, they entered the hut to bask by the fire. They heard the dogs barking and went out, quieting them down, saying: "Away with you, Vusabantu! What are you doing, Nangumuntu? Away with you. Mother!" Then they saw a man carrying luggage, knocking. They saw a tall, dark, brownish young man, greeted him and invited him in. He sat down.

When the young man had sat down he said, "Wo, Mother, darkness has found me. I'm from Gqolweni on my way to Mpukunyoni, and I'm so tired I can hardly stand."

"No, sorry, my child, we cannot offer any stranger a place to sleep in this house because as it is, we don't have enough space for us all. Go quickly to another home before the people there sleep, my child. Mxosheni and you, Ziwede, show him the way to that homestead."

Then the young man said: "But Mother, can't you even give me something to wipe my mouth with? I'm so hungry, and a traveller from another nation. It is said, Mother, that a foot has no rest. Perhaps one day you will find yourself at Mpukunyoni and I'll chase you away as you're chasing me away now."

"Why would I go to Mpukunyoni, being the old woman that I am? What is this young man saying, Qwabes?"

"Perhaps you are refusing food to and chasing away a child of your relative, since I am also born of a Qwabe woman."

"There are so many Qwabes, my child, I am not about to go around digging and tying up all the Qwabe hunchbacks. I would end up full of evil tricks. Manqina of Nonkantshela would be resurrected and I would see him walking with these," she said, pointing to her feet and moving about in the room. The children were watching, and Nokuthela began to look closely at the man who was speaking. Since she was in the dark, she had a good view of the stranger, and pitied him, but when she saw him smiling, she began to be suspicious and said:

"This man, Mother, is laughing. And he said he is from Gqolweni where they slaughter people day in and day out. No Mother, I don't trust him, chase him away. This is a criminal." She spoke and stood up, approached him, looked him over, and then went back to sit in her darkness, observing him again. As her mother shouted, she could see him smiling again. Nokuthela was quiet. Nsikana's mother now started to speak harshly, realising that the man did not move at all; he simply remained where he was. Now she was angry: "Well, I never. Do you see this, people?" Nsikana knew his mother well. He knew that she would start to shout and scream because she did not want a stranger sleeping in her house. And if she started swearing, he knew she meant it.

Nsikana stood up: "Hawu, Mother, you even call on our forefathers, Manqina and Nonkantshela. Is it because you really believe I am a stranger? You really can't recognise me? Who is your son with whom you proved yourself and entered womanhood? I am Nsikana, Mother."

His mother then burst out crying, her hands on her head, as she had almost chased her own son away, thinking him a stranger. Nokuthela then went outside and shouted: "Hawu, here is Nsikana, returned from abandoning his home, my people, come and see." All the family came to Nsikana's mother's house when they heard the cry. They all saw Nsikana and were amazed. His brothers from the other houses came to shake hands because they could hardly believe that he was still alive.

Last of all came the old man, his father, who greeted him uncaringly, perhaps because he had often seen that those who abandoned their homes came back bringing only their bones, or, like some, came back because they were about to die. Or they were called by the inheritance. They would come back and destroy, cause the homesteads to fall apart, knowing no one would say anything since they were first-born sons. They forgot that one could not gain anything by eating and swallowing the sweat, labour, and gifts of other people. That is like eating and swallowing stones of rain, they will turn against you in your stomach and destroy you and your children. Nsikana's father watched and watched this son of his, then took his small knobkierie and left without saying goodbye to his eldest son. He simply asked the boys, Ziwedu and Mxosheni, if all the cattle had come home and if they were all locked up in the kraal. Then he left.

It became known everywhere that Nsikana had come back, and like all those who had abandoned their homes, he had come to be supported. This news was spread by his brothers from the other houses. Nokuthela and her mother were ridiculed because they were not seen clad in beautiful blankets and wearing bangles on their wrists. Nsikana sensed this attitude from his father's family, but was pleased to see that his mother and sister were on his side. One evening he called his mother and sister and showed them the money he had brought with him from Durban. He told them about his mugging and the way he had survived. When his mother cried and wanted to tell the whole family, Nsikana stopped her and said: "Hush, as long as you live, don't talk about this. Mother, and you, ntombi, girl of my mother, I can see that my father's house has turned against me. They take me for a wanderer and the abandoner of a home. As for me, I want to get married, and I will marry a Kholwa girl at that, and will leave my father's homestead to build my own on the mountain. I will build a Kholwa home, and I'm sure that will please you because you, too, are now wearing clothes."

"Where are you going to find a Kholwa girl, because the Kholwa girls of today say we are bhayi wearers, we smell of animal-skins and we are kaffirs?"

"Just keep quiet. I will win the very one that you have never thought of – the girl, who, I hear, lives at Minister Grout's home. I will propose to her and win her over."

His mother kept quiet, took the money, wrapped it up and sat on it. Then Nokuthela said: "No, my brother. I'm afraid that girl is the fiancée of someone else who is highly regarded by the minister; there is no way you can even see and talk to her."

"Don't worry about that, it's my problem," he said, and went to his hut to sleep.

In his mother's hut, his mother and sister did not sleep; they were counting the money that rides on red horses that they had heard is used in Durban. They took it and hid it in the hut's mound. They put it in the drinking pot and dug a hole in the mound and buried it.

They started to walk proudly, not caring what was said about them in the homestead. They also did not care that the father was no longer visiting Nsikana's mother's house, but was now visiting the other houses, especially the second wife and the wives attached to her, the ones who were ridiculing the second senior wife's house. The left-hand wife had become the favourite, and she, too, now walked around proudly.

Nsikana mingled with them all and never minded their actions, but on Sundays he left them and went to church. Because he came with a concertina and was able to play it, he often sat outside and played a song that made the youth of that time go crazy when they were doing the umqhuqhumbelo dance:

```
|| s   :—   |—   :fe   | l   :fe  |s  :—   | —  :r   |r    :r
   Di  - - - - -  da     No - ma-s ng'     - u - yang' - qa

| m  :d  |—   :fe   | m  :-m |m  :r   | d  :d  |m  :m
  mbe-la         wa -    tha - th' - iso - no   sakho  wa - si -

| r   :r  |d   :r   | m  :d  |   :    ||
  shi - ye - la   nga-    ba - nye.            ||
```

Dida Nomasinga you are lying against me;
You take your sin and smear it on other people.

He would play the concertina until his sister, "the long-necked she-goat", joined in, singing loudly until those far away stopped and listened. Since the concertina was a new thing, the people in Nsikana's father's homestead were ultimately curious enough to come and listen to this white man's thing which sang and made people wild. Sometimes Nsikana took his concertina and went away to Mvoti where he visited his friend, Nkomeni, who was the first person he had told about Nomkhosi. But Nkomeni, too, saw only darkness, thinking that Nsikana would not find a way to speak to Nomkhosi. Since he had come back, Nsikana could always be recognised by his song, "Dida Nomasinga" in which the concertina played and was echoed by the mountains. He played it so often that at home they began to say, "That is all, he doesn't know any other song."

When he arrived home, he threw the concertina down in his hut and told his mother about his meeting and talks with his friend, Nkomeni. His mother laughed when she heard her son talk. But by this time the food was ready: perhaps it was spinach or she had brewed sour milk for him. Nsikana ate and went to sleep.

It cannot be denied that Nsikana's mother loved her son with an amazing kind of love. And at the same time his enemies hated him with everything they had. One day he was on his way home and had to cross the river, when he was met by Smonqo, a young man who lived not far from his home, who said to him: "You are crossing this ford during the day; don't you know that the girls are bathing during this time of the day?"

"No, my friend, I did not know that," Nsikana responded.

"I am not your friend. Don't ever again call me friend."

"Sorry, I didn't know, my age-mate."

"I am not your age-mate. Where did we fight that you call me your age-mate?"

Nsikana said: "No, Smonqo, son of Zwelabo of the Nyandus. I've no words then to answer you as I'm like a foreigner in this place; I've been gone for a long time, many things confuse me."

"What! Smonqo? You are insulting me! Calling me by my first name and even the names of my ancestors? I feel like dying, dying here in front of you."

When Smonqo's shouting stopped, Nsikana laughed: "What do you want me to say, Smonqo? You want me to say 'boy'? There's nothing left for me to say." Nsikana said this and then just walked on. When he was some yards away, he looked back at Smonqo: "If there are any of your bathing girls at the river, they should also respect me and cover themselves until I've passed because I don't have wings and I can't fly like a bird."

He said this and walked down toward the river, listening for the girls' voices, but heard nothing. He crossed and realised that Smonqo might have been sent to fight him, or to create conflict for no reason.

Smonqo had a sister who was quite pretty and Nokuthela had spoken about her to Nsikana.

"Nsikana, what is this young woman like?" Nokuthela had asked.

"She is quite pretty, my sister," said Nsikana.

"So, what do you say, I talk to her for you?"

"Not yet, my sister. I am still fixated on this girl who lives at the minister's place. My heart is taken by her. Give me some time. I will tell you," said Nsikana.

"No, my brother, it's a bit too late. I've already thrown in a few words, pretending you sent me. I felt that it would then be an easy walk for you."

"Awu, you've now turned me against the world, Nokuthela. Why do you run ahead of me as though I am a baby? You talked to this girl for me while she's not in my heart?"

"I thought your heart would love all the people I love, and that the girl I would love to be your wife and my sister, you would love likewise. I'm still hoping that you'll listen to me. I feel that this girl you are talking about is not suitable for you. She is out of your league because she regards herself as if she is white, she lives with the whites, and the man she loves acts as if he is white. When he meets us, he doesn't even recognise us, he doesn't even care who we are." Nokuthela said these words and stood up. Her head was held high as if to suggest that she was a young woman who could not be insulted by any young man in this world.

"No. Sit down and let's talk," started Nsikana. "You seem to think that I'm from the rural areas where the white man has never been seen, and where, if he appeared, everybody would be frightened. I am from Durban, where I have lived with white people of all kinds. In Durban, I have seen women who treated their bodies like this one we are talking about, sometimes even better. This white thing is not new for me here at Mvoti. Your words do not frighten me, Nokuthela."

"How do you know if she is going to accept you?"

"That doesn't scare me either."

"Why don't you just talk to this one I'm suggesting; if you marry the one who lives at the minister's, you can marry her as well?"

Nsikana burst out laughing, seeing that his sister was doing her best to steer him towards her friend. "Don't you see, Nokuthela my sister, I'm like a believer, and the law does not allow me to be a polygamist?"

"When did that law begin?"

"That is a believer's law that came with the ministers," answered Nsikana. "The Lord in Heaven, the Ancestor, Mvelinqangi, does not accept polygamy."

"How will that Mvelinqangi see you, as he never comes to the earth? When you die you will go to the ancestors, Shaka and Dingane, as well as our forefathers, where there is abundance. Where a man marries as many wives as he likes, and they brew beer for him, and he sits down and smokes his snuff without worry. Who are you, Nsikana, to abandon the laws of your ancestors?"

"The Mvelinqangi of the Kholwa who I believe in, sees all. He causes the rain to fall, and brings death. He's the one who controls our mythological figures like Nomkhubulwane and MaMlambo, who brings beauty into the world and causes the plants to germinate, and brings love to married people. They are all controlled by Him alone. He's the one who, when He was born, came to the world a long time ago and ruled that those who follow Him should marry only one wife."

"I hear you, my brother," Nokuthela said, and then looked down and kept quiet, as if there was something worrying her that had not been explained. She sat with her hands hugging her legs, as the Zulu girls normally do. Her head slanted to one side, her ears alive to hear what her brother was saying, as if she did not clearly understand it. When she had been quiet for a while, looking down at the ground, she suddenly raised her head and said, "Are you telling the truth when you say the Kholwa do as you say?"

"I'm telling the truth when I say so."

"I also mean it when I ask: do you think you can differ from your forefathers? Look at some of the old men who came with the minister; at first they did as you say – they married one wife – but now they are polygamists because they realised that they were going against their traditions and the culture of their forefathers."

"I don't believe that, Nokuthela, daughter of my father. Even if it was the case, it does not mean the law is at fault. It is they who are wrong."

"As we speak," started Nokuthela, "Makhabeni, who married Lili of Jwabu from Inanda failed, and he married a second wife: the young woman called Nomthombo, daughter of Mdlandla of the Mbambo clan, and he built her a home called Gqu. If you go to the sea today, you will find this homestead; it is there and it is big. Mqwebu married Nozindaba of Sgwebana, from the royal Zulu house, and then he married KaMathambo of Madundube area, and went on to marry Bavimbile of Ngazimbi of the Nyandu clan; Nyokana married Phahlakazi, also known as Gxebe, daughter of Msolwa of the Hosiyana clan, and went on to marry Nomsombuluko of the Qwabe clan. How can I count them? My brother, the Kholwa marry more than one wife. Do I have to mention all of them?"

"Perhaps there are no others." He was adding fuel to the fire in Nokuthela.

"I will tell you about the others like Mbozeyana who ran away to Mdletshana; Mlawu who left for Madundube; and others like Mmangayiya of Mhuhulu of the Zungu clan. All these are alive, you can see them with your own eyes, my brother. How are you going to escape from all of this?"

"It would please me if you could count for me those who have not married more wives as well. Even just two of them would be enough." Nsikana said this and quietly watched his sister, waiting for her reply.

"I do not know them, my brother. I don't think there are any, from those who joined the church first." Nokuthela said this and got up to leave, but her brother stopped her: "*I* will tell you only three, and then not say anything more: there is Ntaba of Madunjini of the Luthuli clan; and John of Nxaba of Mdleyana of the Msomi clan and John of Hlonono of Nqunywayo of the Langeni clan. As for me, I will be one of these, even though you, my sister, do not believe me. Don't cause me an insoluble problem by trying to match-make between your friend and me."

When he had finished saying this, the girl stood up and left, leaving him to agonise about what Smonqo had meant to do to him that morning. Of course, he did not know that Smonqo was involved with Nsikana's brothers from his other mothers. They were the ones who had sent him to cause a fight with Nsikana, saying that Nsikana had said Smonqo's sister was a girl of no consequence, not suitable to marry or even to be in love with. This angered Smonqo so much that when he had failed to provoke a fight with Nsikana, he went back to Nsikana's brothers and told them; they, in turn, assured Smonqo that there was another way he could get Nsikana and demand answers about what he had said regarding Smonqo's sister.

When Smonqo got to think about this, and remembered the friendship between Nokuthela and his sister, it started to dawn on him that Nsikana's brothers were just using him, as they were afraid to fight their brother and just wanted him to fight their battle for them. Thereafter Smonqo refused to involve himself further in this matter, and Nsikana's brothers had to think of another way of bringing their brother down.

As there was going to be a wedding near Nonoti in the land of the Mbozeyanas, they knew that Nsikana would love to come with them, and that he would play his concertina. They realised that if they went with him and he was playing the concertina, they would not stand any chance of impressing anybody with a traditional isigekle dance. All the girls would be taken by Nsikana with this thing from Durban; so they would now be forced to do the modern tamba dance under Nsikana's hand instead. This change of dance worried them greatly, and they did not know what to do.

Smonqo was refusing to play-fight Nsikana, even when they told him that the young man had insulted his sister. They also knew from the past that when Nsikana was still a boy, no one could parry his stick. He was a principal stick fighter among his age-mates in the area. But now he had been gone for a long time in Durban where there was no stick fighting. Even so, no one knew how he would handle a stick and shield, now that he was a grown young man.

What scared them also was to hear that Nsikana had left Smonqo with the words: "You want me to say 'boy' Smonqo? I have nothing more to say." Those words, said by one young man to another, are heavy and full of meaning. If Nsikana had forgotten how to handle a stick and protect himself, how could he call Smonqo a boy? And then he had simply left after he said that. What did all that mean if Nsikana was not prepared to fight? These were all questions Nsikana's brothers considered by themselves, not harassed by anyone, and in the secrecy of their huts, not heard by anyone.

They finally decided to invite Nongunyaza of Manzasengwa, who was a bully in the Mvoti area, to come to the Mbozeyana area for the wedding that was about to take place. They asked Nongunyaza to provoke a fight with Nsikana. Like all disgusting bullies, Nongunyaza agreed to incite a fight with Nsikana and to insult him, and if he showed any stubbornness, he would be hit with a stick that would end it all.

At this time, there were no courts where cases of fighting and blood spillage could be tried. It did not happen that when you hit someone with a stick on the head, the chief's men would go and arrest you, fine you a cow or even kill you. If you hit many people and wounded them, especially on the heads, people gave you praises. People knew that if you were at a wedding and there was a fight, you would come back having beaten some people; so that when the people talked while smoking their snuff, they would say: "What a fighter so-and-so's son is – he's one who hits and the sticks mingle at the top like the smoke of dagga."

That in itself would be interesting. During those times, a man would go to a wedding armed to the teeth with shields and spears, because if a child left home to marry, it was a serious matter. There was wailing as if someone had died, because the child was being severed from her parents, and the child was concerned that she might get to her new home and then perhaps things would not go well for her. Perhaps she would have to feed the kinds of people she did not feed at her father's homestead. Or perhaps she would be as well treated as she was in the care of her mother and father. That is why there was a saying: "Oh, getting married is as complicated as a grass-coil in the open veld," because it was hard to have a good marriage.

Having convinced Nongunyaza to incite a fight with Nsikana, Nsikana's brothers pretended that they had forgotten about him. Others who also did not want him to be suspicious came to him sometimes to talk about the many stories of the war, the old folk tales, and sometimes they begged him to tell them about Durban. Nsikana told them all he could tell them. They asked him why the many young men who went to work usually come back empty-handed. Here Nsikana knew that his brothers were taunting him. He used to tell them that it does not usually happen that a man comes back empty-handed, because even though it may be rumoured that he returned empty-handed, it is likely that he had come back with some clothes worth money, the kinds of things his brothers paid for with cattle. He, Nsikana, had come with a number of blankets his brothers would pay a herd of cattle for. And they could not have clothes like his without leaving home and going to work. He also teased them about their sleeping blankets made of goat skins, and the matter ended in Nsikana's favour.

Days passed, the wedding day approached and Nokuthela never tired of fighting for her friend. But she also wanted to accompany her brother to see this young woman who drove him mad; who closed his eyes so that he could see no good in other girls, and thought about her alone. She considered giving her brother a love potion called umandangaphakathi, that-which-expands-inside; but first wanted to see this girl for herself.

7

It was the Sunday before Christmas. At the first light, the church bell rang at Groutville. It rang so loudly that it echoed in the hills above Mvoti and was even heard at Dukuza where, to this day, Shaka – the-axe-that-surpassed-the-others – rests. Nomkhosi got up, prepared the food, put the pots onto the fire, and washed and dressed the minister's children. But her mind was restless. She was thinking about Thomas and the words he had said about their marriage. She was agonising about what she saw in him, especially his domineering attitude toward the other employees of the minister; and how he told them never to offer a lift to people stranded on the way to Durban. She kept quiet but was thinking. Her mind followed many paths but always came back to the same conclusion: there was no one like Thomas amongst the young men from Mvoti. And the minister liked him. If she rejected him where would she go? If she returned to her father's homestead she would be a laughing stock, and there she would definitely find no one.

When the sun was up she served the food, called the minister and his wife for breakfast, and afterwards removed the dishes and washed them. She wore her best dress for the afternoon service. The church was full, because in those days people came from far and wide. The minister opened the service, and as it progressed he began Nomkhosi's favourite hymn. The whole house rumbled until the hymn was finished; then an old man called Mahawule Nzama led the prayer.

When the service was over, Thomas and Nomkhosi walked together as always. Nomkhosi said to him: "Did you hear the message today? I really liked it, there was something different."

"How do you mean? I think the minister was his usual self." Then Thomas went on to say, "However, I did hear the voices of two young men who sat together; I don't quite know who they are."

"You're right. That also surprised me, because I did hear and liked their voices but don't know them. They were sitting together, but I couldn't tell where they were coming from."

"Yes, they looked very neat and clearly understood our ways here in the white man's land," said Nogiyela's son.

Nomkhosi responded: "Their voices were amazingly good."

Then a boy walked up to Thomas: "There are people who want to talk to you. It's two of them, and they're behind the church building. They are strangers."

"Wait for me here, Nomkhosi," Thomas said. "I'll be back now."

It was the two young men he and Nomkhosi had been talking about. The young men took off their hats, greeted him, then said: "Forgive us, young chief, we come from Nkobongo. We would like to talk to the girl of your home you are travelling with. We have a brief message to pass to her."

"A message for her?"

"Yes, we have a message for her," they said emphatically, and watched one anothers' faces.

"No, please, men. I can't allow you to speak to her. I'm not even sure what your intentions are," Thomas said flatly, and left them.

"Don't leave us like that, friend. Can't you hear we are asking you something?" Nkomeni's voice was rising in anger. Then turning to Nsikana: "See? What did I tell you? This useless boy is protecting her, he doesn't want anyone to see her. By my father's Mantombi who is at Mthethwa, we will follow her wherever!"

"I'm speechless with anger – especially now that I've seen her! I didn't realise she has grown so pretty! Should I now just leave her? Me? Who am I to do that? She promised me, my friend, that she will wait for me, 'No matter when'. I am holding onto those words."

"You can say that again. When I saw her now I realised that she is like those beautifully formed women we met in Durban who would enter the church, and you would hear young men pulling back their legs, watching each other's faces as if saying, 'There it is, you say you are young men, here is a headstrong young woman.'" So said Nkomeni.

As they were talking, people began leaving and the area around the church became quiet. Everybody was on their way home. As for these two young men, their homes were far away, and they had no intention of going home yet. "My friend," said one, "let's go and find out what we can do about this matter."

"Yes, let's do that."

When Thomas had left Nomkhosi, she sat down and waited for him, in the meantime playing with stalks of grass, finely plaiting it to make fine rings to be worn on the arms or legs. When he came back, Thomas laughed and said, "Listen to this, Nomkhosi, that boy was calling me for those two young men who were singing in the church."

"What did they say to you?"

"They wanted to speak to you."

"Where are they from?" Nomkhosi asked, somewhat annoyed, "Wanting to speak to me here in the church?"

"They say they're from Nkobongo. They are now behind the church as we speak." Then Thomas kept quiet as if thinking. After a little while, Nomkhosi stood up and they walked together.

"So, what did you say to them?"

"I just said that would never happen. How can you say you want to talk to a girl while she is walking with me? I just left them there."

When she looked back, Nomkhosi saw that the young men were following them. She kept stealing her eyes away to glance at them when Thomas was not looking. The men waited and watched when they arrived at the minister's house. Thomas was suddenly proud. He felt that he was walking with a real young woman worth the envy of others; but he remained suspicious of those two young men from Nkobongo.

They parted and Nomkhosi went into the house. Thomas first checked on the horses that were tied under a fig tree eating buffalo grass, as they had a long journey to Durban the following day. Then he went to his house a little further from the minister's home.

That same afternoon they visited Nomkhosi's homestead. There was jubilation at their arrival and they were welcomed with delicious food. After that the young women took Nomkhosi away to themselves, leaving Thomas with the other males. Her sisters immediately wanted to know if the rumours were true: that there was a young man from Mhlali who used to be in Durban and who had returned the other day, who was her suitor or her lover. "We want you to tell us because you are the only one whose matters are not known to us. We have a rule of asking about these things. Even about this man who is in the house, we only gathered information from the Nogiyela people and then the ululation. But we knew nothing."

"I thought you knew."

"Who would have told us?"

"I thought you had heard."

"We don't want to hear about the news. We want you to tell us. That is not how it's done."

"Oh, I'm so sorry, I didn't know. And how could I know? I live by myself and have no one to advise me. I'm also a girl like all of you. I felt pushed by love, and I loved; I heard that there is to be marriage and I agreed to be 'asked for'. Now I'm getting married, but I don't know what for."

"Yes, yes, but tell us what you do about these things?"

"You're absolutely right, my sisters, I need to confide in you."

Then her eldest sister, Nontula said: "But first hear this: just this very day, two men came here and were loitering about with intent, and then they asked for water. We gave them water but don't know where they're from."

"I don't know. Suddenly there seem to be many young men travelling in twos here in Mvoti," Nomkhosi said.

"They're not the young men *we* know; we thought they were from the minister's. They left but were clearly searching for whatever they were searching for."

"I can't help you there ..." But she thought it had to be the same young men who had come to church and asked to speak to her. She could not figure out who they were, so she abandoned the matter and focused on the reason for her visit: to ask for wedding gifts from her sisters. She got up and went to Nontula: "My sister, I have to leave now."

"So, what do you want me to do?"

"I'm here to ask for wedding gifts from you all."

"I can't give wedding gifts to someone whose wedding arrangements I don't know, Nomkhosi. If I give you something, I would be spoiling you."

"You mean because I didn't tell you anything, my sister?"

"Yes, but even more: do you think I have any stick or headwear or doek or even ubusenga, wire bangles, from your husband's people? I being Makhwatha's first-born daughter? Tell me!"

"I know you have nothing."

"And now for showing respect. How am I going to respect your future husband's people? What did they give me so that this mouth of Makhwatha's daughter does not call their names?"

she said, touching her lips, shaking her head, pointing to the traditional clothes she was wearing.

"I hear you, my sister. But what should I do?"

"On top of that, he's sitting there and doesn't even know who we are. He talks to the big shots there in the church; as for us who do not wear clothes, we are nothing to him."

"I didn't know about that. I will tell him about it as we go back."

"On my ancestors' graves, Nomkhosi, you are not going back with him. We will escort you the traditional way till you get to the minister's home. As for him, he will just hear you have left. He will see you when you are already too far away."

Nontula then smeared her legs with fat until they shone, threw her shawl over her shoulders, stood up and took her knobkierie. Was she not a young woman who had chosen the Mkhwethus? Mkhwethu was a chief of Mzwangedwa, of the Gumede clan, who was a leader of all of the Qwabe of Mvoti.

She then escorted Nomkhosi with other girls from Makhwatha's home. Nomkhosi's heart was hurt, but she felt a great freedom in travelling with her sisters, rather than with Thomas. They walked with her, crossed the Mvoti River, then watched her walk to the minister's home before they waved goodbye.

As they left, Thomas saw them leaving together as a group – all Makhwatha's daughters – and realised that they were busy talking and that he should not interfere, so he stayed behind. When the sisters returned, they passed him on his way to the minister's home. They saw their future brother-in-law, but passed him without saying a word. He greeted them, and their silence exercised his mind for a long time afterwards.

On Christmas Day, everybody usually came together at Groutville to have a service first, and then a "tree". Here around the "tree" there was the giving of gifts of different kinds. Children, young men and women would sing. A person would write the name of the person the gift was for and that of the person giving it. There would be singing and the calling of people to get their gifts; some men would throw in a few words, praising the work done by the youth.

That Christmas, Nomkhosi, being the favourite in the village, received many gifts, beautiful ones too, the kind she had never received before. Just as she left the church carrying her container with gifts, and was walking with the minister's children, about to reach the minister's home, a girl wearing a traditional girdle came up to her: "My brother said to give you this. I was meant to put it on the tree but I came late; now I am bringing it to you as I was ordered."

"Where are you from, child?" said Nomkhosi.

"I was ordered not to tell my surname, but e...e...eh, to only say the place I am from."

"Where, then, do you come from?"

"I was told the gift will tell you, but as for me, I am from around Nkobongo."

"I thank you my child without a surname, who is from Nkobongo. I am going to call you MaNkobongo." The young girl laughed, said goodbye and ran to join other girls her age from her area who were waiting for her at a distance.

Nomkhosi took the gift with doubtful hands and went to her room. She opened all her gifts and decided to wait before opening the one from the girl. She hurriedly prepared the evening meal, put the children to bed, washed the dishes, closed the mirrors, and did all that needed to be done. Then she shut herself into her room, and sat down with her heart pounding. She took the gift and opened it. It was a black silk handkerchief, on top of which was a little note saying, "No matter when."

Nomkhosi was initially confused, trying to recall if anyone she knew went by the name "No matter when" in Mvoti, but try as she could, she could not recall the name and kept wandering around in the cow's stomach. She left her room and sat on the eastern side of the house where it was quiet. The minister and his wife were also not asleep yet. They sat overlooking the waters of uMvoti River which made long parallel lines on its way to throwing itself into the sea. There was a soft wind blowing, deepening all the beauty of darkness. Lower down where the water formed a current, frogs were croaking, praising God for the abundant Christmas. Wild doves in the forests alternated: some lamented "You let me marry an old man!" while others lamented their chicks being taken by the boys to offer as Christmas gifts, saying, "Malusi and Bongile are taking my house and my children, now my heart says to-toto-totototo." Far away, down uMvoti River where Nongayeyana's homestead was, MaBhengwane cried: "Gudugudu we, MaBhengwane." This was because the language of birds is understood only by hunters, who communicate with them from time to time.

Inside the Grout's house the boys exploded crackers. Smoke filled the rooms while all the children were shouting as loudly as they could, celebrating the day that came once a year.

All these noises were heard by those sitting outside who had ears to hear, except Nomkhosi. She was quiet, looking up into the sky as though counting the stars. That day she could have counted them all, and even seen the smaller ones decorating the Milky Way. Her heart was like a clump of soil thrown to the hill, not reaching the top, but falling all the way down, until it was crushed completely. She did not know what she was doing, and, confused, she repeated the words from the handkerchief: "No matter when." She tried to figure out what the words could mean, her mind anxiously scrutinising the journey of her growing up, sometimes laughing as though there was nothing in the world other than herself and her thoughts. But at last her thoughts had to enter that time: the time when she was a young girl herding her father's cattle with her dog, Nkondlwane, seeing other children going to school while she had to remain ignorant. She saw many of those children had now grown up to be amaqhikiza, leaders of the maidens, the nubile young girls; others were young men, while still others had married. She finally arrived at the point where a certain boy used to shout at her – and she burst out laughing at herself, saying, "Hmn, the way of the world brings pain in a person's life."

From there her thoughts passed on to the time when the minister had asked her to stay at his home. Her heart was grateful that she was finally educated like the others; even if she left the minister's home, she would be able to work for the whites. She pushed away the last thought because it was a wrong thought. Who was she to leave the minister who was like a father to her, who had done so much for her? She vowed in her soul that she would die a child of the minister, respecting him and pleasing him.

Having arrived here, it dawned undeniably on her who the young men were that Thomas had turned away; the ones who had wanted to talk to her in the past two weeks and who also had gone to her home to ask for water. When she reached this point, what she already knew deep down dawned clearly on her: the handkerchief was from that young man who used to shout at her, who went a long time ago to work for the whites in Durban. The child who brought the handkerchief was from Nkobongo, the home of the said boy. It came to her also that she had promised to wait for him to bring her a response, "No matter when".

As she sat there, fear suddenly hit her. Her mind started to race: this boy had come back to remind her of her promise. Startled, she looked around and saw that she was the only one not asleep yet – the noises the children had been making, the voices of the minister and his wife, were long gone. It was dead quiet, her room was the only one with lights on. She took a few steps and opened her door: the handkerchief was spread the way she had left it, with the message, "No matter when." She could not help smiling as she folded the black silk as it had been folded, returned it to the small blue box and put it aside.

She undressed, threw herself on her bed and lay sleeplessly. Her mind was agonising about what Thomas would say if he saw that handkerchief – he was such a jealous man. She was both concerned and thrilled to realise that the handkerchief was a declaration of love from the boy from Nkobongo. Coming to think of it: what had Thomas ever given her? Thomas took her for granted. He regarded her as nothing, as simply a useless leaf, knowing that his power came from the fact that the minister favoured him of the Nogiyela clan. But in the next moment, Nomkhosi said in her mind: "Here is a young man in front of me; he loves me, he adores me, he respects my womanhood; so, why don't I satisfy him?" Then she began to see both of them in that top corner of the mind which sees everything: there were Thomas and the boy from Nkobongo striking one another, fighting over her because she had made the mistake of accepting Thomas's love, forgetting her promise to the man from Nkobongo. Now the man had arrived and wanted what was his.

In her mind, Thomas was saying: "I've asked for her hand, I've introduced myself to Makhwatha." Then Nsikana: "I also am holding on to the word of the lizard of the folk tale: I was told I would be waited for, 'No matter when'. And there is an old saying: 'Beer spills when it has been brewed'. A wedding can be cancelled even when preparations have started. I hold on to that."

She collected her thoughts, then followed a different path of reasoning: "You know what? This is ridiculous. How can it be that a person is engaged but at the same time concerns herself about a man she doesn't know? Perhaps it's not even that boy; maybe he's dead. If he was still alive he would have written to me. I can't reject Thomas, no matter what." With these words she lay down, hoping she had finally caught the mamba by the tail and struck it until it died, and so she fell asleep, taken by those from Sleepland.

It was the habit of the minister's wife always to check whether the children and Nomkhosi were sleeping well or not, and then say prayers, one by one, over each of their heads, before she herself went to bed. On that important Christmas Day, the woman had peeped in and found that Nomkhosi was not in her room. She walked to Nomkhosi's bed and found the rare Christmas handkerchief, with the message: "No matter when." Her head was invaded by suspicion, because she knew that Thomas did not have the money to buy such an expensive handkerchief. Therefore she assumed that it signalled some kind of crookedness in the girl.

Suddenly she heard movement outside, and pulling the curtain aside, she glanced through the window, in the direction from which she had heard the movement. Then she saw Nomkhosi, quiet, on her own, watching the stars. Relieved, the minister's wife assumed Nomkhosi was praying, but just before she left, she heard Nomkhosi sigh: "Can it be that a person is engaged but concerns herself about a man she doesn't know?" The minister's wife left the room and had no doubt that there was conflict in Nomkhosi's heart. She went to bed, her mind now also troubled because she believed that Nomkhosi was seeing a man other than Thomas.

The woman told the minister, but he suggested that they keep quiet because he was convinced it would resolve itself. They kept their eyes peeled, and angled their ears on every side, but

Nomkhosi showed no change in anything she did, not in the way she walked, not in the way she swiftly worked, even when she was sent to the river, or fetching firewood; there was no news of any young man approaching her, or stopping her to talk about proposing.

So who sent the handkerchief? Where did Thomas get it? If it was indeed from Thomas, why was she not wearing it? Maybe she was waiting for the wedding day so that she could wear it as a headband. Or else, her father, Makhwatha, had got it for her. These were the thoughts of the minister and his wife.

8

One afternoon, the minister was visited by a young man who came to ask about religious matters. He was accompanied by an adult woman. After the young man saluted him, the minister brought chairs out so that they could sit on the veranda. The young man spoke: "Mfundisi, I came here about a minor matter. I'm asking for advice. I'm a bachelor, and I want to get married, but my journey is filled with darkness. I'm from around Nkobongo."

When the young man mentioned Nkobongo, Nomkhosi, at that stage inside the house but within hearing distance, listened. She stopped and watched the young man closely and saw the deep scar above his left eye; she also looked at the young woman with him, and decided that they were just people who wanted the minister to marry them.

"So how can I help you, my child?"

"I am asking about the Kholwa wedding, Mfundisi."

"Yes, my child, it is time for us to reap the fruits of our work. As you say you have come from Nkobongo with this girl, it would be good to remember that marriage is supported by the ancestors."

"I don't understand now, Minister. I assumed that ancestors are for us Zulus and we are being told to get rid of them."

"No. I am referring to the ancestor of the ancestors, Mvelinqangi, who is the lake-with-a-plaited-headcover-inside, he is Simakade, living up high in Heaven," the old man said, pointing at the sky which was blue and cloudless.

"Now I hear, Minister."

"My child, you must keep your promises to all people; you must not forget them."

"Minister, your word is hard. If you made a promise when you were young and said you will keep it when you are an adult, do you remain obliged by it?"

"Yes, my child, it is indeed necessary, unless it is a promise relating to something bad."

Working inside the house, Nomkhosi coughed: she could hear every word and felt herself hooked into the conversation between the white-haired minister and the young man.

"It's common with you Qwabe boys to claim that you are popular and have relationships with many girls in all the hills and the mountains. You play with girls, forgetting that polygamy is not allowed for the Kholwa. All these women you end up not marrying, I do not like that, I don't marry a young man like that."

The young man was touched: "Minister, since I was born, I've never been in a relationship with a woman. I grew up during hard times when the school over there on the hill at Shaka's Rock had just opened, where the homestead of Mdleyana of the 'White Starlings' was situated. I left home in the morning every day, and came back in the afternoon. Then my father forced me to leave my education and go to work in Durban."

As he said that, Nomkhosi came out of the house carrying a bucket of water to pour onto the flowers. She came out and saw this young man with her own eyes, and with shock realised that it was indeed him, Nsikana. But who was this one he was sitting with, and were they to be married? At once she felt herself flooded with envy: she saw that this young man was civilised; he also had cut a line parting his hair, was wearing shoes, and carried a hat in his hand. The girl did not suit him at all, but then love did not choose where it fell, and you could not understand where it fell. You found a good-for-nothing young man with a pure wholesome girl, and then you could only look and say nothing more than, "Oh, my father!" After emptying the bucket, Nomkhosi walked tall and elegantly as she passed them on her way back to the house. She wanted the young man to see her. When she arrived at the door she turned, wiped dirt from her feet, and caught the eye of the young man. She found that his eyes were absolutely fixed on her, as if saying: "Can't you see, silly girl, I ooze water for you like the meat from an animal that has not been slaughtered but that has died from sickness. I sleep on the ashes for you!" She turned, this daughter of Makhwatha, and entered the house, and Nsikana could hear the sound of her working.

He continued: "My father forced me; caught me by the neck and I was sent to Durban. Even there I lived with bachelors, cooking, not having time at all to play around. But during all those years, Minister, my mind was here in Mvoti. I wanted to marry a girl of my land, who grew up in our area and in the sight of my parents. Now I am here to ask you, Minister, to help me if you can." Nsikana said this confidently because he had seen that the girl was affected and was coming out of the house to encourage him.

The minister was listening carefully: "Your speech, my son, catches me like the rod that catches the fish in the water. It affects my feelings; it seems like the first time that I have talked to a person and heard him open his heart like this to me. I will help you, no matter what." The minister promised – so the young man heard the promise, the young woman with him heard the promise, and the astutely cunning one, Nomkhosi, also heard it while pretending to be working.

"No, Minister, I don't want to be misunderstood: my story is very difficult, it's weighing heavily on me, and perhaps will weigh heavily on you too, Minister."

"I've said that I'll help you. You can speak."

There are many things we promise without looking ahead; we tie ourselves into knots, sometimes heading towards evil, sometimes towards good. There are always dark shadows in a person's path, and we are prone to error.

"When I was still a boy I was promised by a young woman who lives with you here, that she would wait for me. She gave her promise using my own words: 'No matter when.'"

"Who are you referring to? You mean the girl who passed here carrying the bucket, who poured out water there a short while ago?"

"Indeed, that is the one I mean, Minister, if her name is Nomkhosi of Makhwatha, there near the upper Mvoti," he said pointing at the homesteads, including that of Nomkhosi's father.

"No, now I don't understand your story, my child."

"I'm telling the truth, Minister, I mean that very girl – is it not so, Nokuthela, my sister?"

"Yes, brother it is so. That girl is Nomkhosi."

"I am speechless, my children. Speechless. And powerless."

"Let me finish my story, Minister," said Nsikana, knowing that he had stabbed the minister with his own spear, and it was now in his entrails and could not be removed. "When I was in Durban, I saved myself; I went to work for money. I came back and now am here to inform you of my situation. I know, Minister, that this girl is engaged to one of the young men in your favour, but I also come to you presenting my case because I was promised by this girl herself, many years ago when we were young, that she would wait for me, 'No matter when'."

The minister's head was swirling, and he did not understand all that the young man was saying. He realised that he had promised to assist the young man, and that long ago Nomkhosi had made a promise to this young man. He also remembered that his wife had told him on Christmas evening about a handkerchief on

Nomkhosi's bed with the message, "No matter when." All this dawned simultaneously on the minister. He folded his arms and stroked his beard which was becoming white, starting from the whiskers. His eyes were fixed on the spot where Nomkhosi had poured water from the bucket. He stared there for a long time, dead quiet. The young man saw that the minister was deep in thought, and said to him: "Minister, I'm leaving now. My name is Nsikana Mbokazi, son of Bhoqo from Nkobongo. I greet you, Minister."

As they were saying their goodbyes, Nomkhosi sneaked to the river to fetch water. She had heard all she wanted to hear. When she came back from the river, there they were, coming towards her, the brother and sister, and she did not know how to handle the whole situation; it had all gone to her head too, and weakened her bones. She strengthened her courage and headed towards them as if she did not know them at all. She walked straight towards them in the middle of the road, balancing the bucket on her head without using either of her hands. Then she hit a clump of grass, now using one hand to keep the bucket still. She kept walking, this young woman, whose eyes looked as if they were shaded by the smoke of dagga, who was as beautiful as though she had been bathed in the milk of an Angora sheep soon after she was born. She strode down the middle of the road, and Nsikana could only stand and watch, desperately wanting to say something but not knowing what. He stood speechless. When she passed them he turned to watch her: her clothes swishing this side and that side, lightly sweeping her calves as she walked; it was not the wind blowing them, but the force of her body. Then this son of Bhoqo burst out laughing with boundless joy, and Nokuthela said: "This is it, my brother, you always said that if you got an opportunity you would approach her, why wait? There she goes!"

But Nsikana kept quiet. He was thinking about Thomas who wanted to marry this woman who suited him so. When he was about to succumb to the sudden anxiety caused by this young woman walking away, Nokuthela's words rang in his ears: "This is it, my brother, you always said you would approach her!" He stopped dead, watched his sister and saw her grinning at him. He turned to the girl and saw that she was moving up the hill to her home, having taken her hand off the bucket. He ran and caught up with her, but did not block her way, as was the custom for local people.

He took off his hat and said: "May I speak with you, child of God, you who, while we went down the hill to cut grass to build huts, you went up to the white houses, painted with clay from overseas. I beg you, nkosazana, for just a few minutes."

Nomkhosi stopped and felt her joints loosening. A thought that perhaps this man was bewitching her flitted across her mind, but when she looked at him, she found that he was wearing clothes, had no horn on his neck and had not grabbed her by the hand. Nomkhosi stopped short and was the one speechless now.

"Forgive me, nkosazana, I've been meaning to talk to you for a long time but I didn't get the chance. Are you Nomkhosi, daughter of Makhwatha from Mzwangedwa?"

The young woman said: "I am."

Nsikana said: "Do you recognise me?"

The young woman said: "Who are you?"

Nsikana ignored that and looked her steadily in the eye. She flinched, as she had held her eyes up, expecting him to tell a story.

"On Sunday we asked to talk to you, but you were walking with a respectable man so we waited. When we asked him, he refused, saying you do not have time, you are in a hurry. As for me, maybe you have forgotten me. Let me not even say, maybe, let me just say, you have forgotten me," said the son of Bhoqo, having finally gathered the courage when he saw that the girl was standing and listening and was in no rush to walk on.

"Not forgetting you, but who are you?" asked the girl while she laughed at him, playfully sarcastic.

"Now you're pretending. Even your smile says you're pretending."

"No, it's true. Ever since I came here to the minister's home, I have never seen anybody like you. Also, you are not from around here," she said, while her fingers pulled a nearby piece of high grass and played with it; she began chewing it, her foot writing on the ground like someone caught off-guard, having nowhere to escape.

"Oh, here you are, saying I'm an unknown man! Where's your dog, Nkondlwane? Are you still able to herd livestock and to milk? Let me see whether your hands are still as rough as before! And today you say I'm an unknown man?"

Nomkhosi kept quiet. He had caught her out, and she somehow felt that mentioning her days as a herder was belittling her, downgrading her, and she began to feel apprehensive. Too late, Nsikana realised that "rough hands" was an unfortunate expression: "You, Nomkhosi, child of God, who said when we were still children down there near Mandelu's place, you said to me, child of my King, you said you would wait for me, 'No matter when'. Now I have arrived, I'm grown and a young man, I am this tall. And you too are grown to be a young woman, you are that tall. I'm here to collect what is mine, and you, too, take what is yours."

As he said that with a calm voice, Nomkhosi took a step back and removed the bucket from her head. She sat down on a clump of isikhonko grass, and listened quietly. Further down the road Nokuthela was watching the two. They were like two armies battling each other: then the one from Bhoqo retreated, then again it was the one of Makhwatha retreating. But when she saw Nomkhosi sitting down on the grass, she knew that her brother had somehow overpowered this girl who had passed them with long strides, full of her Kholwa attitude. She felt happy that her brother had dared to approach her, but then that happiness turned to annoyance: how dare that girl, while being courted, simply pass them by. She, the one and only Nokuthela. The famous Nokuthela. And the girl passed her without even a glance or a word. She imagined this girl taking her brother and going to Durban with him for good, or perhaps the minister taking them overseas, leaving her, Nokuthela and her mother suffering again. She asked herself if it would not be better for her brother to be loved by a girl who was not so civilised?

Nomkhosi was sitting down, without words, her legs weak. Nsikana asked: "Do you now recognise me?"

"It took me a long time to recognise you, but I'm in no position to accept anything you say. I'm somebody else's fiancée."

"Are you the fiancée of that man you always walk with? Yes, you see I knew that. I came to you knowing that. I heard it while I was in Durban. Zulu sayings tell us: 'No quarry-digger can dig for another; the beer gets spilled when it has been brewed.' As for you, I have never heard that it has been brewed, or that the people have already been invited and asked to soak the sorghum."

"I don't think it will help you to hold on to this matter in this way. My time is up, I have to leave, the minister will need me soon." She got up and took her bucket, but Nsikana quickly picked it up and put it securely on her head. To Nomkhosi, this kind act brought back many things. She marvelled at the fact that Nsikana had not aggressively blocked her way when they first met now. And instead of leaving her alone with the bucket, he had taken it and put it on her head. This was so different from Thomas, who simply watched as she was struggling with a bundle of wood.

Nsikana took her hand and it made her happy, because he simply held it, he did not grab and pull it harshly, he held it where it was and then spoke: "I'm not prepared to step aside for that son of Nogiyela. Since I've waited till now, I'm holding on to the promise that you, child of my King, made when we were children still playing with clay, moulding small cows and people. Even if you reject me, I will follow you. I will follow you from sunrise to sunset. I will follow you while you are as beautiful as you are now, like the fine sands of the sea, your cheeks full and smooth like gourds, until you have the wrinkles of grandmothers. You will look back and see me coming towards you, and you will look ahead and hear me following you with firm footsteps. You will get tired and sit under the shade of fig trees, and I will wait for you to get on your feet again and follow you. I will follow you until you die, I will pursue you in spirit until I hear you say – yes, Nsikana."

When he said the last word he let go of Nomkhosi's hand. It fell back on her dress and she was too flustered to do anything. She slowly turned and left, then Nsikana walked away and did not turn back. After they had parted, Nomkhosi thought about what he had said, that he would follow her everywhere; she did not quite understand what he meant by saying that he would follow her even when they were both dead, both spirits. She asked herself if it was true that there was a place where people corrected their sins when they were dead. If that was the case, then Nsikana was right to say he would follow her even when she was dead. If not, then this stranger was insane. But even as she said that, her mind was overwhelmed by a feeling that – no, what this young man said rushed straight to and flooded her heart and was staying there, refusing to evaporate – unlike the sermons of the ministers who admonished people for losing their way.

As she came up from the river towards the house, not feeling the walk or the bucket on her head, her ears were tuned to the concertina playing down near the river: "Dida Nomasinga, he's lying to me." It played softly and then stopped, and then the young man would take over and sing, and Nomkhosi continued listening; she could not do otherwise. She was old enough to understand that a man who spoke like this and played the concertina like this was an unusual man. He was different; he had a magnetism, and when he left, he left a kind of loneliness behind, so that one felt that he should always be around and not go far.

She arrived home, went round the back to put the water down, and then checked if the minister needed her for anything. The minister was still sitting where the two visitors had left him. He was still staring at the ground, his heart broken because he had assumed that the young man was going to marry the young woman who had escorted him, and he was more than willing to officiate at their wedding. In those days, people did not consult widely, or they went to the courts; the minister would just marry those who came, put his hand on them and they would leave. Faith was not as strong then. Those who belonged to the mission came with their families ululating for them. The ones who came from afar would be married by the minister, and, after the minister had finished, a traditional representative would ceremonially perform the customary "asking", asking whether the bride loved her husband. But trouble-makers at weddings would sometimes, for no reason, beat the representative with sticks, and the "asking" would be abandoned. Going to the courts to get married had only started recently, when people began to realise the importance of writing.

Nomkhosi put down the water, her heart pounding, and she went to play with the children, trying to avoid thinking about things. The minister sent her to call his wife who was at a meeting. As Nomkhosi had seen and heard everything, she had no doubts about why the woman was being called. She remembered that on the evening of Christmas Day, she had stayed outside and forgotten the handkerchief on her bed. Since the minister's wife always entered her room before going to bed, she must have seen it. Besides, the minister's wife usually asked her about the gifts she received, but this time she had not done so. Why not?

She answered herself: "The woman knows my story. If not, she will soon know its intestines."

The minister's wife arrived and she and her husband talked, walking up and down in the yard, at times standing still, as if in disagreement – something that was very rare. They were speaking that language of the foreigners, but what they were saying could be translated into our language as follows: "Yes, this young man says his knot with Nomkhosi is older, the one with Thomas is new."

"But how does this matter involve us?"

"We are involved because this child stays with us, and Thomas belongs to us."

"Let us leave them alone. They will sort themselves out."

"I can't! I have made the mistake of promising to help this young man who was here."

"How could you do such a thing? This could get you into conflict while you are an ordained man of God!"

"I didn't realise he was referring to Nomkhosi, and didn't get involved intentionally."

"So how did it happen?"

"This young man came with a young woman, and I spoke, assuming that the girl he came with was the one he was going to marry. Then I promised him that I would do everything to make his wedding both beautiful and Christian. The young man asked me to promise and I did."

"So, how does this involve Nomkhosi?"

"It turns out Nomkhosi promised this boy before he went to Durban, she said she would wait for him 'No matter when'. The boy now has come back to remind her."

"Have they spoken with Nomkhosi?"

"Not in front of my eyes."

"Oh, now it's clear that the handkerchief I saw at Christmas was from this boy, as there was also a written message, 'No matter when.'"

"But what are we going to do?"

"No. This matter is easy, Minister," said the woman. "I have studied the ways of the Zulu nation. Do the following. Call Makhwatha, the father of the girl, and explain this whole thing to him. He is the one to sort it out. In fact, he won't even sort it out, he will refer it to the girls, the young women, of his family. They are the ones to come up with a decision. He will act according to that decision, and we will abide by that too, but let us not involve ourselves in this matter."

"You are absolutely right, you of my own," said the minister, having regained his strength; for he had seen no way of getting out of the mud he had got himself into. "You're right. Whomever she rejects between these young men, we will marry her to the chosen one. Because how can we know? If this one called Nsikana could stay in Durban for three years and come back uncorrupted, and carrying so much money – how do we know, perhaps he's the one the Almighty could give us to carry forward the work of the Lord among his flock," said the minister. They started walking, the minister having had his knees strengthened on this issue. "But there is one thing we have to do: we have to pray, asking that the one chosen will become one of our staff."

As it was already quite dark, it was decided that a boy would be sent the next morning to call Makhwatha to the mission, with Bantukabezwa, who was like a brother to him. Indeed, the boy woke up in the morning, crossed the Mvoti River and went to call them. He found they were not at home, but, as izinduna, they were off to drink beer at the homestead of the chief, Mkhwethu. A message was left with MaMthimkhulu and MaCele.

When the sun was about to set, the old men returned. Makhwatha was grey-haired due to his heredity, and Bantukabezwa was bald. They arrived and were seated on the small, ornate chairs at the minister's home. Their headbands had been well prepared and their imitsha suited them well.

No one knew what the conversation was among the three men, Makhwatha, Bantukabezwa and the minister. All that was known was the reason why the minister had called them, but in the lines of a poem recited at Mzwangedwa many times after the incident, we do get a clue:

:m	|—	: .m	d	:— .m_1|s_1	:s_1	s_1	:m	|—	:r
Wo		wa⁻	nge -	nz'uMa	mla -	mbo	Wo.		wa -

S	:—.m|s_1	:s_1	mr_1d_1
nge -	nz'u - Mamla -		mb.

We ask you, Makholweni,
And you, of Gqolweni,
You lobola-ed her with money
But she is lobola-ed by cattle,
We cry for our fathers' cattle,
Wo, MaMlambo let me down.

The story-tellers say it was composed on the day of umemulo of Nontula, Makhwatha's eldest daughter. She composed it herself and gave it to the young women of her father's homestead to sing and to dance to. As time went on it spread throughout the region. Everyone was crying about MaMlambo.

9

During the times when the missionaries and ministers arrived, the world became divided along the lines of family, religion and civilisation. Those who converted soon after the arrival of the ministers started to separate themselves from those who were afraid of believing. These heroes of belief called themselves Nonhlevu. They had great and widespread fame at that time; they were the ones in charge of education. As a result of their enlightenment, they soon bought land for farming and for building. They heeded the advice of the minister, who had warned them about the time to come; he enlightened them about the time that lay ahead when Shepstone[3] and others would divide the land of the Zulus among many scattered chiefs. He explained to them back then, why it is that now, today, we wander all over the land without owning anything, only being grateful for the rising and the setting sun. He showed them the land when it could be bought with one hump-backed ox; with just that one ox you could section off and buy a piece of land which today would cost thousands of oxen.

In all the places where the ministers started the work of the Lord, it was clear that the descendants of their converts, their offspring, were not following in the footsteps of their fathers. They even looked down on education. They were like a cock, perching on top of the fence, flapping its wings, crowing, looking down upon all the land; forgetting that soon it would fall down to the earth of the millipede, like all the other chickens before it, and that in the end it, too, would boil in water. And so, too, would the offspring. And other chickens would be kept in their place.

It's true, Nomkhosi was the child of a heathen, but she was a Nonhlevu, just as Nsikana was. In the land of his people he dressed like the heathens if they were going to traditional functions. He put on a big feather from an ostrich, knitted to the feathers of a guinea fowl, a bird that cries loudly as it runs, and other feathers of the dark ostrich. Then he carried a huge shield made from a black-and-white-coloured ox. On his shoulders hung strips from the skin of the blue monkey which were tied at the neck with that of the genet. He could not have done otherwise, for it was necessary to show that even though he behaved like a white man, he had not completely jettisoned the ways of his own people; not like today, when some people claim to be following the whites but they cannot fit into the life of whites, and then they say they are black but they know nothing about blacks.

It was a great day when he dressed himself like the young men who had become foreign to him, the day of the wedding at his cousin's home near the sea where the Mbozeyanas live today. They travelled as a group of young men and women, cutting through the Mvoti as the path went through the village, but no one recognised him among the many young men. Nsikana was a very adept dancer and performer; so much so that many young women from "outside" were attracted to him, wondering whether he had a lover; of course, being popular with the girls made him unpopular with his age-mates and others older than him.

He had been disliked by those from his father's homestead the moment he arrived. They pointed fingers, "Wo-eya! This thing is full of himself. Ever since he came back from Durban, he thinks he's white." Some of the girls, too, intensely disliked him, saying that he did not approach them because he regarded them as pagans, smelling of animal-hide blankets and red clay.

Things became worse when it was known that he was friends with a young man from Mvoti, the place where the Kholwa lived. In spite of all this, Nsikana did not open his mouth, he just kept quiet and associated with them all; those who were no longer talking to him, he made a point of visiting.

It was on the day of the traditional wedding in Mbozeyana that the young men conspired against him and wanted to pit him against a muscled young man of the Ndimande clan. The problem began with the ukugiya dance. When the Mbozeyana group were performing, the young men urged him to go and dance from his side; no matter what he did, they praised him so that the man from the Mbozeyana side would get angry. Because when he was angry, he would hit any opponent with his stick. They knew that nothing went past this young man and came back alive:

> Ngongoni of Water-Being-Milked,
> Nongunyazana is hard
> Because he caught even the lumps.

When the dancing began, this Ndimande man went forward and danced with his mouth wide open, showing his teeth. He danced and his bloodthirstiness was aroused. As he danced, the saliva drooled from his mouth, and the women almost cried because they sensed that if one man from the other group went forward to dance, blood could be spilled. When he was about to finish, Nsikana was put on. When he made his first move to start his dance, the young man laughed and went and pushed him with his shield. Nsikana stopped and looked at him. But instead of fighting him, the young man of Ndimande laughed and said to Nsikana: "Hawu, they are sending me a little boy though I am this big? They offend me. Go back, boy, I do not intend to fight with young boys, go back."

All those who were watching were surprised. They thought Nsikana must have a very potent charm, the one used by whites to tame mad people in Pietermaritzburg. His brothers wanted him to be beaten here, and to leave him behind when they returned home, so that he would disappear without a trace. When it was time for the bridal party to dance, Nsikana, this son of Mbokazi, outdid himself and he was the centre of attention once again. The old men from Mbozeyana, who were not jealous, called him, and made him sit among them before they asked him if he was married and who his father was. He answered: "My father is Bhoqo of the Mbokazi clan."

Then the men said: "Come closer, boy, and drink from this calabash." Nsikana went on to drink with respect: he drank and then put down the calabash, wiping it all around with his hand.

And the young women of Mbozeyana and Dlozi and Nonoti, too, were amazed by him. Later, on their way home, they gossiped about him, saying great men are born in Nkobongo. This kind of talk was heard many times, and it infuriated his brothers.

The time for the serving of food and beer came. The men divided those who were there into groups according to age, and the areas from whence they came. The young men from Nkobongo were offered a hut, and were served the beer there. They were served by the woman of the house who was assisted by another woman. She said it would be best if the one who finished should bring the calabash to her so that she could refill it for them. She said that because she wanted to talk to Nsikana.

Since Nsikana was now isolated, the young men made it a point that he was the one to finish so that he could take the calabash to the woman who was serving them. They began to laugh at him as he stood up and carried the calabash, but he did not take any notice of that. When he arrived at the hut the woman who was serving them advised him: "My child, I don't even know where you come from, neither do I know your parents. But I pity you. I was listening to the young women of our side saying that they pity you because they heard the young men from your side gossiping about you by the river. You will not make it home alive if you do not take my advice."

Nsikana was surprised and said: "Oh, what are you saying, Mother?"

The woman said: "Yes, it is true."

Nsikana then said: "Let me take this beer to the hut and then I will come back to hear this properly."

"Listen well now, my boy. There isn't much time. I am about to go and serve the others."

"No. Wait, Mother. If I delay they will suspect and come looking for me."

"Go then. I will wait for a while."

"I will find an excuse to come back here." And indeed, he took the beer in the calabash and returned it to the hut, then pretended to go out to spill urine-water, and found the woman.

"I'm about to give you advice, my child. Take your belongings and steal away home; pretend that you are sick or in a hurry to be in time for a certain ritual at home. The sun is still up."

"Hawu! What are you saying, Mother?"

"I've said it. By sundown you'll be at Dukuza, and by the time people go to sleep you should have reached the village of the Kholwa at Mvoti. There you can sleep in the home of a grey-haired white man people refer to as Minister Grout. All those stranded at night he welcomes and treats well; even ones like you and me, who wear traditional clothes, to him there is no difference."

"I've heard you, Mother, thank you so much. Where are you from, so that I will remember you wherever I am?"

"It's not important that you know my name. Just take me to be your mother and be content with that; remember me when you are with your own mother."

"I am indeed grateful, Mother. Let me go while there's time."

Nsikana thought: this had already been hard for him: to leave home to accompany his cousin, but now to leave his cousin's wedding and run away from other young men; but worse still, to go and sleep at Grout's home while so traditionally clothed. The minister and Nomkhosi might see him, and all he had been trying to build would be destroyed. But what benefit would staying have, as his own brothers were going to kill him on the way? He was quiet when he re-entered the hut, drank some more, and then ate like the others.

When they went out and scattered, and the evening dance was on, Nsikana took his shields and pretended to go to the river. He travelled alone through the forest, going upward until he reached the path to Mbozamo. He was running like an antelope. By the time the sun set he was facing Dukuza. The land was still wild in those days. People believed that, on the way to Dukuza, there were tokoloshes and wild cats that had owners who used them for witchcraft. Even today, there are people living at Mvoti who have been carried off by the beasts of the dead. Even I have seen them, but then I cannot insist and swear that tokoloshes and wild cats exist or do not exist. Because I don't know this, my people, we will leave this issue to the coming generations to investigate, to ascertain their validity or otherwise.

Nsikana travelled. When he reached Ngudwini, his hair started to tingle, his knees weakened and he could not walk. He thought that perhaps the woman had lied to him, intending him to get hurt. His head became confused, and he started to ask himself how his own folk could want to kill him when he had not quarrelled with any one of them. Look now, he was in danger of dying alone in the wild.

Just then he saw something that looked like a baboon. It stopped in front of him, stood, stared at him, and then ran and disappeared. After a careful look at it, he realised that it was an antelope on its way to graze on the bluish-red grass of the veld. His mind told him that the grey duiker does not eat where there are other animals, which meant that the tingling of his hair must have been caused by this animal, its eyes staring at him. He ran on until he crossed the water of the Mvoti River when it was already very dark.

The minister's homestead was near the river, and he began hearing children cry and play in the yard. In the homes nearby, he heard the ox-wagon drivers calling their oxen and the sound of the yokes as they hit the ground; and how the drivers told the boys to herd the oxen to graze at MaNdelu. He wished he could go home, but he was dead tired. He dragged himself on, and made his way up to the minister's homestead. Just as he approached, he saw the minister sitting down and wished he could run away, but he had already been seen by him. He went forward and asked for a place to sleep.

The minister asked where he came from, and this unrecognised man said: "I'm from Nonoti, nkosi yami."

"So, where are you headed?"

"I'm going to Durban, to the land of the whites; I'm going to search for work and money."

The minister called Nomkhosi, and asked her to take the stranger to the visitors' hut as it was very dark outside, and give him food. Indeed, Nomkhosi took the stranger and asked him: "Where are you coming from and where are you going on such a dark night, Father?"

"I am from Nonoti and am going to uThungulu in Durban."

"All the people seem to like going to Durban. I had a cousin who was working in Durban. He came back bringing a lot of things for me."

"Hawu, you are right, child of God, you are not just talking. It shows," said the stranger.

"How can you tell that a person has cousins from Durban?"

"Some I can see wearing clothes from the white man's land, and the young women do not tie up their hair in topknots but wear black, sparkling head-coverings." At this Nomkhosi smiled but flinched, because this man somehow excited her. And the stranger himself knew what he was doing: adding wood to the fire, wood that would burn and spread the fire.

"Are you going to wake up and leave early in the morning?"

"Indeed, child of God. You are so pretty that just speaking reveals your beauty, nkosazana. I wonder who your parents are."

"No, I belong here at the minister's," Nomkhosi responded, thrilled because it felt good to be appreciated by a man from far away in Zululand, and to have him telling her about her beauty. But if it had been someone from her own area who had blessed her with such flattering words, she would have been very apprehensive. Indeed, Nsikana saw that the weasel was wooing the hen by showing it its tail, and the hen did not see it was a trap.

"Hawu! You are so pretty, if only you were born in Zululand, I would have thrown in a few words by way of proposing, even though I am this old," he said pretending to be an old man, and the girl fell for it.

Nomkhosi then fetched the food, still holding her head high and walking quickly. She came back and gave it to the stranger waiting for her in the dark. As the man was eating in the hut, Nomkhosi was standing outside, waiting for the dishes, looking down uMvoti River, her mind preoccupied, as if she had forgotten that there was a man intently watching her. Nsikana pretended to eat but his mind was elsewhere, as he watched this young woman whom he now believed loved him, judging by the fact that she referred to him as her cousin to other people. He was amazed by her beauty; it seemed that she was a black angel coming from above to tantalise him. Indeed, if you love a girl, when she accepts your love she is an angel in your heart. And how much more so if you intend to marry her? Her beauty will grow and strengthen until it blooms like flowers when you are married. All this Nsikana saw, and he ate, though oblivious that he was eating.

He watched Makhwatha's daughter standing near the door, as tall as a willow tree in the heart of a thicket. He saw that she was tall, brown, with big round eyes, full-breasted and slim-stomached like the bees running on the flowers. She was full from below the waist down, like all the girls from the Qwabe area. Her hair was as black as if anointed with soot, and plaited in two long strands, falling this side and that, like the tassels at the end of cows' tails. Still quiet, Nsikana felt like saying: "Bone of a snake; stab the one you hate; you are close to kicking it; go on, ntombi, this is me, Nsikana, the one who has been crying about you."

He decided to keep his words to himself. He was lost in the thoughts in his head when he remembered the handkerchief and said: "It's just nothing, 'No matter when.'"

Nomkhosi was startled and said: "Are you finished?"

He said: "I am about to finish, nkosazana."

"So why did I think I heard you speak?"

"Oh, I'm thinking about the journey still to come to reach Durban. I know that even though I'm this tired, I'm going to walk till I get there, by the name of my sister, Nokuthela."

Nomkhosi laughed, then kept quiet and folded her arms on her chest. Her mind was lost in her own thoughts again. Nsikana watched, kept quiet, and was amazed by her complete beauty. He felt like standing up and looking for some light to show her who he was, but then chose to swallow his words when he remembered his loin covering, the shield, and the crest of feathers; he saw that he would be cutting himself on wood if he approached her now.

So he said: "I am done, nkosazana. Hmn. I am grateful for your kindness. Even though I'm this tired, I will have the strength to wake up in the morning and walk. Perhaps I will see you again. I'm very grateful."

Nomkhosi took the dishes and left with them. The stranger said: "Go well, nkosazana." They parted, with Nomkhosi having discovered nothing, and suspecting nothing about the stranger who was sleeping in the hut.

Thomas passed by the hut when he was coming from his work, as it was his habit to visit the people who were sleeping there, and to wake them up the following day before they commenced their journeys. He came and said: "E! Mister, where are you headed?"

The stranger said: "I'm going to uThungulu, where there is plenty."

"Where are you from?"

"I'm from Zululand."

"How's Cetshwayo's leadership? We hear that he's now the bull?"

"He's just leading, but it seems as if he will resemble his uncle Dingane by being mean."

When Thomas started speaking in the dark, Nsikana quickly realised that this was his rival, so he pretended to be too tired for talking. He feared that if Thomas discovered him he might dirty the water upstream so that he, Nsikana, could not drink any more. Thomas left and stopped near the minister's house. Nsikana coughed, and pretended to be singing. Not being a child, he could see that the young man was calling his girlfriend. And indeed Nomkhosi came out of her room, looking over her shoulder as if she did not want to be seen. They stood together for a while, speaking in hushed voices, but Nsikana could not hear what they were saying. He could feel the anger in his heart and remembered that it was this young man who had refused to let him talk to Nomkhosi. He thought about what it would be like to knock him down with a stick and separate him from the girl whom he also wanted. Or else just beat him to death, for there would be no court case. But then his conscience said to him: "Don't kill." The heart of a Christian prevailed here, and the one of non-belief died. He sat down again, as he had by then stood up – consumed with jealousy, unable to tolerate the sight of the girl he loved being so amiable with another man.

As Thomas and Nomkhosi stood there, Nsikana again coughed, went outside and walked around the hut, trying to ignore what was happening. By the time he came back, Thomas was leaving, but suddenly Nsikana, this son of Bhoqo, felt that hope was leaving him. It was as if he was hitting his head repeatedly against a rock. All his hopes evaporated like fog in the rising sun. It left him with an emptiness, and he talked to himself like a madman. Later he promised for a second time that he would fight for her. He would throw himself down in front of her, talk to her when he was in a better position, and remind her of her promise. Then he remembered: she had not returned his handkerchief. This caused some hope to flicker. If she wanted to reject him, she would have returned the handkerchief, according to tradition. Even though living with white people, she would need to follow those prescriptions in rejecting him.

10

"I do hear what you are saying, but this thing you are telling me is difficult. I can't open my ears for it."

"Believe me, I love you, Makhwatha's child, I love you when I'm standing, or when I'm sitting; all these mountains remind me of you. I don't sleep any more, I'm always dreaming about you."

"I don't use any love potions, so how can you dream about me? Don't make people misunderstand."

"Listen carefully."

"To what? You are my brother-in-law?"

"Forget about that, that's *my* business, don't get involved in that."

"I *should* get involved, because my father would kill me if he learnt that I had come out at this time of night for you."

"But do you really think I am interested in Nomkhosi? What is she? This Kholwa thing? Who is her mother? Look at me!"

"Yes. That's all very well, but you *knew* that when you proposed to her. But today you see stains on my sister, Nomkhosi."

"Don't. She's not your sister."

"How can I deny her? She *is* my sister; and stop breaking my arm, let go of me," said Ntombinjani, who was born of one of Makhwatha's houses, but not that to which Nontula belonged. When Thomas saw that she kept arguing with him, he twisted her arm. The girl began to cry.

"I'm telling the truth when I say she's not your sister, she's something that was found. I don't love her any more; all I want is you now. Just imagine the life you could have with me; you would live a better life, leave these huts behind and move to the houses of the Kholwa over there. How good it is to be a wife of a Kholwa!"

"You are trying to lure me, you are turning me against my father's house; you want to come between us and cause a conflict that would never end."

"No. My words are true. You will never hear me talking about Nomkhosi, I don't love her any more. There's no reason for that, except that my love for her has ended, Ntombinjani."

Having said that, Thomas took hold of the necklace on Ntombinjani's neck and held on to it. Ntombinjani tried without much conviction to make him let go of it, but Nogiyela's son held on. Opening the hook clasp, he took it from her, and put it in the pocket of his trousers. He took her hand and stood, looking the girl in the eyes, and saw that she was pretty; and she too glanced at him and felt tired. He let go of her hand and left. He walked proudly, this son of Nogiyela, as he now had two girlfriends.

He actually had no real intentions towards Ntombinjani and was just playing with her. The blood of Shaka rushed up in him. It was Nomkhosi whom he was interested in, and he amused himself with this other girl, knowing that Nomkhosi would not reject him, no matter what. He calculated that it would be easy to win Ntombinjani if he approached her by unkindly criticising his fiancée, staining her with the story of her adoption by Makhwatha. And indeed, Ntombinjani was taken in easily.

When she arrived home, Ntombinjani was afraid when she remembered that her sisters would ask her about her necklace. Therefore she met with her elder sister, Phikiwe, who did not get along with Nontula, and told her what had happened. Phikiwe approved, but warned her to keep it from Nontula because she would destroy this budding relationship. So Thomas hid next to Phikiwe's mother's house when he came to see Ntombinjani.

They used to go out together at night when no one could see. Their mothers knew about it, but were also covering it up. They did not like the prospect of a foundling getting married before the real children of the home; and on top of it, marrying a gentleman from the white man's land! They desperately wanted Ntombinjani's affair to succeed.

It seldom happens that in a big homestead all the members of the house get along. There are always those who support evil. Some of the young girls demanded to know about the absence of Ntombinjani's necklace, especially those who were of her age and knew all about her. In the end they smelt the truth and heard from the herd boys that the brother-in-law was now visiting Phikiwe's house, and always left with Ntombinjani. The boys told the story with so much conviction that they were believed by the girls, but the girls wanted to see it for themselves. So one night they stayed outside and waited. They saw their brother-in-law entering Phikiwe's mother's house. Then they saw him leaving and Ntombinjani waiting for him outside the homestead. Thereafter the girls were quiet, and left, not talking to each other.

One of them said: "What is so good about proposing to *one* girl and marrying her? It would be better to throw oneself into polygamy than be made a fool of like this!"

"That's true, my sister, because in polygamy you know that there are many of you. You will all take care of the man, instead of struggling in the house, cooking for a man and thinking you are the only wife, while there are others more important than you who take from him what they want."

"I feel like killing myself," wailed another girl. "What are we going to do?"

"Let us report this matter to Nontula tomorrow morning."

"This is all Phikiwe's doing. She's involving Ntombinjani in it because she wants to be the leader of all of us, though she is not from a senior house. And how can she lead us with that double-edged tongue of hers like a monitor lizard's?"

Yet another girl: "I want to be led by Nontula who is going to get married to the chief, and we, her sisters, will have dignity and be known as the young women of a man who has a name in Mzwangedwa."

At dawn the next morning, this girl left and accompanied Nontula when she went to wash herself. When they were scraping the soles of their feet, she said:

"Sister, I have to tell you something, because I'm concerned it could tarnish our name."

"What now? Has one of you lost her virginity?"

"No, my sister, it's about Ntombinjani. Last night, we were just standing outside and then saw our brother-in-law leaving Phikiwe's house, and walking with Ntombinjani."

"So what's wrong with that? She was walking with her brother-in-law?"

"No. We have heard that their relationship is no longer that of in-laws. You don't hand over your necklace if he's just your brother-in-law? Didn't you say we should not give our necklaces to young men who propose to us? We think they are having an affair."

They finished washing their feet without Nontula saying a word. The girl knew that she was not going to discuss it with *her*, but she was relieved that Nontula did not get angry, so she cleaned her feet, unconcerned and in silence. Nontula did not say anything. The matter ended there and the girl did not raise it again. Speaking later to her friend, they decided: "Let's keep quiet and we may hear something burning." Indeed, they kept quiet and stayed alert. The next night they saw Thomas arriving again at his usual time at Phikiwe's, and then leave, meeting Ntombinjani. Nontula did not take heed of this matter. She ignored it. She locked it away in a hole.

121

11

He woke up at dawn in the mission's hut, this son of Bhoqo, and hit the road straight to Nkobongo, not wanting to be seen in traditional clothing by the people of Mvoti. He arrived at home as the sun rose, entered his mother's house, asked for food, ate, and slept the whole day without talking to anyone. Then that night, singing voices were heard from far away, wailing, "Dida Nomasinga, you are lying to me." They sang, coming home from the wedding where Nsikana's life had been threatened. The young people who had stayed behind came out to welcome them as they all arrived – an army.

Those at home had not seen Nsikana arrive that morning. When some asked about him, those who had gone with him to the wedding responded that they had left him at the home of his relatives. It ended there; they talked about the wedding and what it was like, they said how beautiful it had been, and praised the Mbozeyanas for their good hand at serving food. Everybody was happy.

Later that morning, they saw Nsikana well dressed and playing his concertina on his way to see his friend who lived in Mvoti. He did not tell anybody what had happened, and the people at home did not notice because he was the kind of person who liked keeping to himself. He arrived at his friend Nkomeni's, and spoke for the first time: "My friend, I went to a wedding at Nonoti, but people almost killed me there; I was only saved by a woman who advised me to run away."

"Hawu! And you are glad to run away from other men?"

"What are you saying? You've never seen people hating you so much that it becomes a matter of life and death; looking at you with the eyes of a cheetah, licking its lips and flicking its ears as though it's spotted an antelope?"

"Even so, friend, run away? I would die there, by the name of my sister Ziwelile," said Nkomeni Khuzwayo, whose praise name was Witchcraft-Induced-Thunder. He said this and spat on the ground.

"Indeed my friend, I ran away. But there's still good news to come."

"When they were chasing you, did you jump over trees?"

"No. I was just no longer there."

"I'm still bothered, and wish we could go and beat them one day when you are not afraid."

"Leave that, my friend. When I was coming back, I slept at the minister's. Beast of premonition! And I saw this young woman."

"Oh. There we go again! Why go to the minister's at night, wearing skins? You've disgraced yourself with the young woman, considering that she is what she is."

"No. Don't be so impatient. I was a wolf in sheep's clothing in the dark; I pretended to be a nobody. I was allowed to sleep in the hut, and she was sent to offer me food."

"And when she arrived you talked to her, presenting your own case! Goodness, what were you thinking!"

"No, I didn't! I purposefully asked her calculated questions and told her things that made her fail to discover my true identity, until that useless boyfriend of hers arrived. At that point I felt like confronting him: what are you doing here? But of course, I was the one to be asked that question since I did not live there."

"If you were me, you would have thrown a clod of mud at him, then pretended to be asleep. If he didn't run away, another one directly on his body. How would he have known it was you? Wo! We have been travelling this world."

"No, my friend, I kept quiet, trying to figure out if she does, perhaps, really love him. Whether she saw my gift. Or whether she's just playing with him."

"What did you find?"

"No, I don't know, it looked to me that she loves him. The journey has become too hard for me. But I long to talk to her. She told me about her cousin who sent her things from Durban. I think she liked my handkerchief."

"Friend, it doesn't help to keep guessing. A young woman is a young woman whatever we say. She is also capable of playing people. Haven't you heard it said that young men have killed each other over a woman? Even here, they have just killed a man who is the only son of his mother; they hit him with a knobkierie on the temple and he died on the spot. Just because of a girl who loved two boys."

"You think it is the same here? She loves me and then goes on loving her old boyfriend? How can she do that when she is a believer, and she has not even told me how she feels?"

"No, I'm not saying that. I'm just telling you things that *do* happen here, not what you think *should* happen."

"This is terrible, Nkomeni, you of the warrior, I don't believe in operating like this; it would make me die, die before seeing the world."

"Then do it, my friend. I can see that you really love this woman. Do it."

"Do what?"

"Listen to me, or keep quiet until you die: go from here to Makhwatha's, just go straight there."

"What is this man saying? Have you ever heard of this being done? Are you trying to make me look like an idiot?"

"I said hush till you die," said the one whose praise name is Witchcraft-Induced-Thunder. "Leave here and go straight to Makhwatha's. Arrive there, salute, and ask to talk to the first daughter of the homestead; her name is Nontula. Explain yourself to her. Hang your story clearly before her."

"I hear you, old friend; you are speaking like a man now. Before that, you were just excited."

"No one will suspect you if you ask for Nontula, because she's a fully grown young woman. You can see for yourself that here, at the minister's, you won't see Nomkhosi, because the minister doesn't want to see strange men walking about in his yard who haven't been sent for anything. Even if you come to the workers, it won't help because you won't find her. Even if you wait near the river, how will you know that the minister is not there?"

"That's true; the minister has to be respected; you can't look him in the eye, even if you meet him on the road riding his horse. How much more if he finds you talking to the girl from his house! This is very hard."

"I am giving you the only plan to win this battle. If it fails, we will have to give up, or go to Sandlasikhulu, the Big Hand, to have him foretell with the bones, have her dream at night, and create disagreeableness between her and this son of Nogiyela."

"You are joking there, my friend, because I made a vow when water was put on my forehead that I will not put my faith in deceitful things, and will forsake evil acts."

"I know that, Nsikana. But I am trying to help you. If you don't want my help, then I wash my hands of it all. Let's say Nontula doesn't like what you tell her, or else when she talks to Nomkhosi on your behalf, the girl eats her with her teeth, what will you do?"

"I'll keep my head down, pack my luggage and go back to work in Durban. Go and never come back, because I cannot bear to see Nomkhosi marry another man. Or wait, perhaps I can go straight to the minister and ask him to keep his promise, or at least allow me to talk to Nomkhosi properly. Those are the only two ways I am prepared to follow."

"Indeed, it is difficult. The battle can be fought in different ways, but I, I would take out a horn now," he said drawing a magical potion from the stalks of the hut's roof, "then we would point the horn, and spit this way and that way, call her name and then sit down, and see if she won't enter through the door and you will see her with your own eyes."

Nsikana said nothing as he watched his friend demonstrate how a woman could be bewitched. Thanks to Nkomeni's powers of description, he found it intriguing:

"Is this all that you do, and then the girl loves you? How does the charm travel to where the girl is, while you are here and she is far away? I know there are some lies about this witchcraft of yours."

Then they parted and Nsikana headed home, hoping to come back the next morning to go and see Nontula. When he arrived home, he found that his sister, Nokuthela, was burning with anger: she had given up on the girl who, having taken her brother's handkerchief, continued to walk with Thomas. Only girls who have no morals would do that. She talked to her mother about this, voicing her worry that the girl had accepted her brother's gift but still walked with his rival.

In their discussions, they were forgetting one important thing: according to Zulu law a boy should never give anything to a girl. But if a girl gives a boy something, she shows that there is a spark burning for that boy. So how could they blame Nomkhosi for not having given anything to Nsikana? Perhaps they, too, had heard about the ways of the white man's land, where girls receive gifts from young men who are courting them, and in that way show that they are about to accept a man. So who was wrong in this matter? Why did Nomkhosi keep the handkerchief, though she was aware of the ways of the white man's land? Or was she holding back from giving anything because she understood the ways of the outside people who were not believers? Which of the two ways was she following?

12

In Durban there were many whites, most of them English, doing different jobs. It had become clear to everybody that they were here to stay; they were no longer just visiting. And those people who could see for themselves saw that things had changed. In the north, the white Mbuyazis[4] from Durban were married to black people and were living a Zulu life, having stretches of land under their rule. At the same time, there were whites who had become really powerful in the heart of Zululand, like Shepstone[5]. There was another white man who married a Khoisan woman, Gwendoline. His name was John Dunn, and he had arrived as a visitor in Zululand and been accepted by the king, Mpande[6]. He later became Cetshwayo's hunter and lived as his subject.

Just as some whites were the subjects of black people, many black people came closer and closer to the whites in Durban. The whites came with habits learnt from their mothers and fathers, and the blacks came with what they had learnt from the Zulu nation. They met at work, and blacks would often try their best to please whites, even to the extent of spilling their own blood, preferring to fight against their own race rather than being seen as traitors by white people. Blacks did all this to avoid persecution by black rulers in Zululand who ruled with blood, just like all the leaders of the nations not yet influenced by religion.

Ndongeni sacrificed his bones and headed for the waters of the harbour to accompany Dick King, until he arrived at Hini[7], not expecting to be praised by either the white or black poets, doing it all to prove his love for the one he had chosen as his chief. It was like that also with Ndabankulu, son of Nkontshela of the amaNgwane. They were hunting with the whites in the forest in Nkandla, where a white man shot a leopard in the stomach and it did not die, but hid in the bush. This white man carefully stalked the leopard to finish it off at close range, but just when he was near to where the animal had hidden near the entrance to the bush, it leapt to attack him. Ndabankulu saw it first, and ran between the white man and the leopard while it was in the air, so it fell upon Ndabankulu, savaging him, ripping open his stomach and spilling his intestines. By the time the white man finished it off, it had thoroughly mauled Ndabankulu. It was said that when others ran towards him, he was already busy putting his intestines back into his stomach. They held him down and stitched him up with thread made from the small crown tree, but Ndabankulu did not even utter a sound of pain. He lay in bed for a week and after that woke up and carried on as before. The white people saw this and recorded it, noting especially the spirit of dedication of a black man willing to sacrifice his life, sacrificing his bones for the white man.

White people saw all this bravery coming from the house of the black man and wondered why these people, who were so fearless and powerfully built, just wilted when faced with the power of sangomas and their predictions. Even when a hero had killed in battle, if he was called to the assembly of diviners dancing this way and that, carrying white-and-black tails of the hartebeest, this heroic warrior would look down, as do all really courageous brave men, but he would then begin to shake like the stem of a tree blown by the soft wind from the clouds. The whites wondered how that was possible.

This tendency remained with people, even when they had converted to the church. The weight and power of darkness did not remain behind in Zululand, but simply followed them. If a young man said, "Accept my love, child of God," to a young Zulu woman, she would not say, "Oh yes, young man, I accept" just because they were in the white man's area. Even Nomkhosi herself was not about to just accept Nsikana saying, "Yes, Nsikana," when he came from Durban, asking for the love he had left with her when they were still young. What would she do with Thomas whom she had accepted when the sun was bright, and all the people at Mvoti knew?

And Nsikana had his own worries regarding Nomkhosi, especially when he began to believe that Nomkhosi really loved Thomas.

Thomas heard the rumour that Nsikana had visited the minister; when he asked what he had come for, Nomkhosi said she did not know. And others came to tell him that this young man from Nkobongo had spent a long time at the minister's, accompanied by his sister, and then went down to the river where Nomkhosi herself was. They asked Thomas why Nomkhosi had stayed with Nsikana for such a long time, even taking the bucket from her head, and sitting down herself, if Nomkhosi was not giving Nsikana a chance to talk to her? If this girl had nothing to do with Nsikana, then who had told him that she was at the river?

Those of Mvoti, like Zisini, asked these questions, as they read between the lines of this story, understanding something although it had not been told to them. They questioned Thomas until it finally dawned on him that the girl was leaving him for Bhoqo's son in Nkobongo. He immediately became consumed with fits of such jealousy that it overwhelmed all his thoughts, and he began strategising to find a way to see the girl alone before she rejected him. He desperately began to think of the many herbalists who might help him with potions to vaccinate himself and to bewitch Nomkhosi so that she returned to him.

It was difficult for him to bring himself to go to Manzesengwa, Water-Being-Milked, to have Jevuza divine for him what potions he should take; it was even harder for him to cross the Mvoti River to Qwabe to see Manzohlanya, Madman's-Water, to take his charms; because it would soon be heard by the Kholwa that the most trusted of the minister's house visited diviners, and was partaking in witchcraft.

In the heart of Durban there was a man called Sihlangusinye – One-Shield – who apparently divined in a new way, combining the knowledge of the Zulus and the Mpondos down at Faku's place, with the knowledge of the diviners from Lesotho in Moshweshwe's land who bewitched with lightning and thunder, plus the knowledge of the whites, who had crossed the seas and come to Durban and Zululand. In addition to using the fat of a black person, he-who-basks-in-fire, to confine someone to one place so that that person, especially a young woman, did not move about, Sihlangusinye also used the fat of a white person, he-who-comes-out-standing, to hold the matters of a man together, so that all went well for him.

Sihlangusinye had great fame; people came from far and wide looking for his charms, bringing cows and horses as payment. People did not know that some of Sihlangusinye's power lay in his use of a big mirror that he put in front of his client. This person would watch himself in the mirror and see himself talk; it would weaken him tremendously, and his voice would enter his own ears while he saw the lips in the mirror moving; and then Sihlangusinye would speak with a frightening voice, asking what the person was looking for. The client would answer, shuddering. Meanwhile Sihlangusinye would have prepared the charms, and if he had to bewitch a woman, he would ask: "Do you see that shadow you have been talking to on the mirror?"

"Yes, I saw it, Father."

"That is your ancestor who is supporting you in your matters. This charm that I'm giving you, I received it from him, because your ancestor knows everything you want."

If the person asked: "Since he knows what I want, why doesn't he tell me?" Sihlangusinye usually said: "That's because you're dirty, you're not suitable."

"What has dirtied me?"

"You've lived with the whites for too long; the African charms don't work with you."

"What does that mean, you who speak with the ones on top and those underground?"

"Shut up. Don't ask so many questions, lest you don't leave this hut alive. You may die before you see your children and your siblings."

"I hear, diviner, I hear." When he tried to leave, Sihlangusinye, holding him by the hand, had one question: "Your matters will get better through the fats of that-which-comes-out-standing. Do you hear?"

Then he would give the person a small bottle with some fat that smelt of rot, and advised him to keep smearing it on his forehead whenever he was going to speak to the girl.

After some time, people started to ask themselves what that-which-comes-out-standing was. Some of the people who knew things, and who were living with Sihlangusinye at Msizini near the harbour, said that-which-comes-out-standing is simply another name for the pigs from the sea called dolphins, because they often come out and peek at the world with their tails above the water. Others said they were lying because that-which-comes-out-standing refers to the horse, which had so much power that it ran with a person on its back. At last some discovered what this term meant, and they spread the knowledge among people. In the remote areas far away, herbalists started to arm themselves in preparation, especially for white visitors. The herbalists would gather certain men who were known to be criminals, order them to catch a white person, remove all the fat from and in his body, and bring it to the herbalist.

The herbalist would take this fat, fry it, and then put the liquid in bottles. But around Durban, people who were caught for having killed a white man were killed as well. Because of these death sentences, the herbalists there waited for the funeral of a white person, and then, in the middle of the night, would dig up the grave, take out the body, and remove parts that were needed for treating people.

This did not end there: after some were caught and arrested while digging in the cemetery, a white person would be identified and then taken and killed where the white government would not find him. The people who were doing this kind of work were called the Ones-Devoid-of-Hair. Yes, many people became rich due to the fat of that-which-comes-out-standing; even people who had been nobodies prospered and became respectable men, with multitudes of cattle and big stomachs that touched the ground. Sihlangusinye had this fat; he was like a big container from which people drew.

Thomas found himself standing in front of Sihlangusinye. It was the first time he had been in Durban.

He had woken up one day and told the minister that he was leaving for Durban the following day; he would go with the ox-wagon which was to pick up a minister in Durban who had to come and inspect the religious work that was being done among the Zulus. Before leaving, Thomas had said: "How lucky I am that I'm going to Durban!" He planned to go to Sihlangusinye; he could give him the power to bring back Nomkhosi, who by now did not even talk to him for long periods. These days, when she went to her home across the Mvoti River, she went alone and was no longer escorted by Thomas.

Thomas left with the drivers of the oxen early in the morning, and they broke their journey at oThongathi. There they found many young men who had let their oxen free to graze and who were telling all kinds of tales. Some were coming from Durban, having long been gone; they were discovering a number of things for the first time, for example, that roads had been made for wagons, due to the amount of traffic. Others, especially the youth, were crowded together, talking about things concerning them. They asked from those coming from home if so-and-so of such-and-such a surname was still in love with so-and-so. And that young woman who was so high when I left, how tall is she today?

Thomas sat down listening, until one of the young men said: "How tall is that girl of Makhwatha, the girl who was found?"

Somebody asked: "Which one do you mean?"

Another who was listening said: "Is there another girl who was found by Makhwatha apart from the one he found the day that unity was destroyed between Mpande and Dingane?"

"That's the one I was talking about."

"I left when she was still young, and threatened that when she was older, I would come after her."

"If you are talking about the one who was found, you should see her now. You would never close your mouth, my friend, you would be speechless."

"What do you mean, friend?"

"It's the truth, you won't be able to look at her. You will faint – by my sister Mantombi's name."

"Do you think I would fail, even when I'm wearing the beautiful breeches I bought to show off at the church some day?"

"What are breeches?"

"Oh, so you are still stuck with loin-skins? We are now wearing clothes from Durban, my friend."

"Don't laugh at me. Just tell me what breeches are?"

"No, you are still on your way to Durban. If I tell you, you will spend all your money and come back with nothing left to pay lobola for your fiancée."

"You can refuse to tell me what breeches are, but you are going to Mvoti where you will meet Nomkhosi!"

"Who's that Nomkhosi?"

"So you're quick to ask how Makhwatha's daughter is, but you don't even know her name?"

"If she defeats me in this way, I will approach her in another way. And so I will continue."

"There's no other way with that young woman, because even if you come with all your family's charms, you will still fail."

"I'm not coming with my home charms, because there's no herbalist there, but will go as I am; if she rejects me I'll come with that-which-comes-out-standing."

When he said "that-which-comes-out-standing", even those who were not interested in this conversation strained their ears and came closer; several pairs of eyes met one another across the fire and waited for an explanation of that name.

"What? What are you saying, friend? You will come to her with 'that-which-comes-out-standing'? Where are you going to get it, being like this?"

"What do you mean, 'being like this'? You are rude, disrespecting me in front of young men while we are telling a tale!" He was full of anger as he said this, and the others made a great deal of noise trying to hush the man from Durban.

"No. I meant no disrespect. I say this because I see you are dressed like the Kholwa; you are not carrying any bags and you are not wearing charms made of horn around your neck like all the herbalists. I'm intrigued: looking the way you do now, where will you get the fat of that-which-comes-out-standing?" said a Zulu man who did not understand the ways of the Kholwa. He said this and kept quiet, jaws shut.

All this time Thomas was watching, consumed by his thoughts. The first thing that scared him was to hear Nomkhosi mentioned out of nowhere, in this wild place where he did not know anyone. He thought that Nomkhosi was his secret for whom only he competed with Nsikana. And now he was here in the wild, and had found a crowd of young men talking about her. He thought that, indeed, the name followed its owner: this girl had, as a baby, been found on the day the alarm was sounded that unity had ended, and her name, likewise, was spoken in public all over the place. He felt very angry, but remained near the fire, not even moving, lest the others noticed that he was here; perhaps someone who knew that he lived at the minister's place might blow his cover. It was fortunate that, by the fire where Thomas was, there was no one of his wagon, because they might have blurted out that they knew Nomkhosi, and that her fiancé was here in one of the wagons; this might cause the men who were going home to court Nomkhosi to kill him for that reason.

Sitting there, his thinking began to change. He found himself looking down on Nomkhosi, while the image of Ntombinjani rose into his mind. He saw Ntombinjani making him known to many women at Makhwatha's homestead; and he recalled that visiting the houses where Ntombinjani was born, they all took care of him: he was brought water to wash his hands and given food to eat. But when he arrived with Nomkhosi, he was always taken to the upper houses and treated like a nobody, and the young women there, like Nontula, did not care about him at all. They were only interested in him subjecting himself to them:

he, Thomas son of Nogiyela, who was known all over Mvoti, Mzwangedwa, Qwabe and Nodunge!

When he had finished praising himself, he returned to the question that if Ntombinjani was so much better than Nomkhosi, why were the young men there then talking about Nomkhosi and not Ntombinjani? And why was it that out of the whole army of daughters of Makhwatha, the minister had chosen Nomkhosi? When he started to see Nomkhosi again in his mind, walking with her firm step, her hair plaited into thick cords, not done like those of the betrothed girls who wore topknots, he, too, was overcome by the sleep that had come to the people who were basking by the fire; as they were lying there, they had felt the heat entering through their legs, and they rubbed them until they had dark flower spots on the skin from the fire's warmth. Just as he was falling into a deep sleep, but still vaguely hearing what was said, he heard the words that-which-comes-out-standing, and all hope of sleep was gone. He tried to listen closely to what was said about this remedy, but the young men quarrelled and all was lost.

They slept with the wagons facing opposite directions; the ones heading to Durban had their shafts facing south, while the ones going from Durban to Zululand faced north. The oxen were tied by ropes, lying down chewing the cud of the insinde grass of oThongathi. Often you would hear one of them lowing, others rattling their yokes, others horning each other, and others swishing insects with the tuft of hair at the ends of their tails. They slept in the wild; the air was cool, bringing peaceful sleep. When it was dead quiet, you would hear far in the darkness of the night an owl calling, "Mgidugudu – weh!" And the other would respond and say: "Quiet, morning is near. Quiet, owl."

These birds spoke like that until the morning star appeared down by the sea, and those drivers who were eager to sleep at

Dukuza that night inspanned the oxen and set off; and after that, those who were going to Durban. The man who had threatened to pursue Nomkhosi left and Thomas saw him disappear into the distance until the wagon he was on became as thin as a little speck of shadow between firmament and earth. His heart was hurt, and he became homesick, urgently wanting to go home with this young man who wanted his fiancée.

When the sun was up and very hot, they were passing Mdloti, and decided to stop to rest down at Mawoti, so that the oxen would get water and good grass to graze. In the afternoon they put the oxen back into the yokes and took off. By nightfall they were crossing uMngeni River. Thomas saw many houses close together, and in all of them, lights that could be seen from far away were burning. In some houses, he heard concertinas playing, and young men grumbling, some dancing, and others just singing while they cleaned off their feet because they were coming from work. When he arrived at the wagon-station, Thomas started to wonder about where he could find Sihlangusinye.

For the first time he sat down and opened his heart to the driver of the wagon whom he had been ignoring since they left home.

"I am going to ask you, Ndosi, to tell me something that is worrying me, because I'm not well in my spirit; don't be misled by my quietness."

"So how can I help you?" said the driver. "We are just useless people."

"It's just a minor thing, it isn't big."

"Spill it out then."

"You know, Ndosi, that at home I have a fiancée, Nomkhosi."

The driver said: "That I know for a fact."

"My heart is not completely happy about this fiancée."

"What do you mean by that? What we know is that 'they are swept away with the stubble' – she and the son of Bhoqo at

Nkobongo; and that she is the one not happy with you," said the driver.

It hurt Thomas acutely to realise that people were aware that Nomkhosi was about to reject him. He did not want to let the driver see that, so, summoning his strength, he changed his story, pretending he had not heard Ndosi's words.

"I've heard rumours that – as you are familiar with Durban – there is a herbalist whose name is Sihlangusinye. Do you know where he lives? Can you take me there?"

"What do you want with Sihlangusinye, because you and I are believers, we vowed that we would never associate with the herbalists who divine? What would the minister say if we tell him that you have been to see Sihlangusinye?"

"You can go to the minister and report to him if you like, but he will never believe what you say about me."

"Is that what you think? Don't lie to yourself, son of Nogiyela. I'm older than you are." The driver stuffed his pipe, struck a match, lit it, and smoked as if he had never spoken, or he had forgotten what he was saying. Then he said: "Just tell the truth, that you want Sihlangusinye to help you bring back your girlfriend who is busy leaving you."

"You are completely mistaken. I want to get the charms to treat my injury, as the pain in my foot has never completely healed since I fell from the minister's horse. Awu. Do you think I would go for the charms to bewitch someone?"

The two men, Ndosi and Thomas, set off, and after a while they saw an old man walking, followed by a young man striding along and crossing the roads, passing houses and trees. When they began to smell roasted meat and saw black people's huts appearing, the driver of the minister's wagon said: "We've arrived."

"Now which of those houses belongs to Sihlangusinye?"

The driver said: "Do you see those three houses? Turn after them; and the one you will see in front of you is the house. Go straight to it and knock on the door; you will find the one you want inside."

Thomas went as told, sweat dripping from his forehead and cheeks, feeling hot all over his body. He had had to walk swiftly to keep up with Ndosi, who did not want to come to Sihlangusinye. He refused to go inside, and said he would wait for Thomas outside the homestead. Thomas found the house and knocked with the long finger of his right hand. He feared he might wake the people living nearby.

Those inside did not hear, so he knocked harder, and a loud voice answered: "Who is knocking at this time of day?" Thomas said nothing, afraid that if he answered it would seem that he was shouting. Sihlangusinye spoke again and said: "Who is that?"

"It's me, Father," Thomas said.

"It's you? What's your name? Don't you have a name?"

"It's me, Father, I'm a traveller, I am here to see you; I'm from Zululand."

"I am sleeping now, I don't want to see anyone," Sihlangusinye said. The noise of the grinding stone inside, grinding charms made from herbs, could be heard.

Thomas stood outside feeling helpless, thinking that he would not have time to return the next day because he would have to search for the minister who had to return with him, and they had to leave on time to spend the night at oThongathi.

Thomas knocked again and began hailing Sihlangusinye: "Oh, You-who-talks-with-the-ones-underground-and-above; you who, when your eyes were opened, were made to face down so as not to see what you see. Open so I can enter. I, who am a weary traveller who needs your help at this time of day, I have no other time than this." He said this and was amazed as to where he found such courage and from where he drew such words of praise, because he was no praise poet. Suddenly the door opened. He slowly peeped in, then entered and squatted next to the door. At first, his eyes did not see anything. He looked without seeing anything except for the fire that was burning at the far end of the house. Then his eyes adapted like those of a cat, and he saw a man sitting with his legs spread; between his legs was a flat stone and the other one was round, for grinding herbs and charms. At his sides lay bundles of charms. Thomas saw many pots arranged according to size and number, and above him many horns hung, clearly filled with potions: there were feathers of birds drifting above, covered with soot and smoke. He wiped his eyes and now focused his gaze on Sihlangusinye himself, who seemed unconcerned and continued grinding his herbs on the stone between his knees. When he looked at him closely, he saw that on his head Sihlangusinye was wearing a head-ring, and that there were few hairs on his head.

He again studied the house, and saw spears and shields hanging from ropes in the section opposite the doorway, and in another section there were ropes holding sleeping mats. He turned and, with a shock, his eyes met those of another man who was sitting near the door, who had been staring at him all the time. He realised that this was the man who had opened the door. He could smell the odours of the herbs that were being ground, as well as those which had already been ground, and the fats of different animals, but he heard nothing except for the noise made by the grinding stones.

After a while Sihlangusinye asked: "What is it you want?"

"Oh, Father, I came to you because my fiancée is running away from me. I have 'asked for her', but now she wants to accept another man."

"Now you want to offer her to me, while I am this old?"

"No, Father, I am here to invite you to advise me on what can be done." He began to realise that Sihlangusinye was a man who had a sense of humour and kindness. Then the herbalist said: "It's now dark, my child, I cannot work when it's dark, because the man I speak with is right there." As he was pointing, the man who was at the door stood up and went to turn the big mirror to face Thomas, and then turned it away from him again. There was nothing amazing to Thomas about the mirror because he had seen a bigger one at the minister's home.

Then Thomas explained his story, and Sihlangusinye stood up and shook the dust from his loin-skin, and picked up a bag with small bottles. He filled one of them with some fat, then took another potion which was powdery and put it in another bottle. He explained what was to be done with them, took another one, sprinkled some of it in a snuff box and gave it to Thomas. He then asked how many cows Thomas had brought.

"I don't have any cow that walks on feet."

"So, what does the one you have walk with, a head?"

"No, Father, I have money, three scotchmans."

"It's all right. Take it, boy, and put it where all the rest is kept." The boy took the money, and Thomas said his goodbyes. Sihlangusinye said: "Those fats are of that-which-comes-out-standing, so your matters will stand up always." Thomas had, indeed, been expecting at least to hear about that-which-comes-out-standing, and when, at first, it had not been forthcoming he began to suspect that Ndosi had brought him to the wrong house. He took his potions and put them into his pockets. When he stepped out, it looked as though it was day because of the stars that were still giving light. He breathed deeply and relished the cool air that blew softly, as he had been locked in the darkness with the smell of Sihlangusinye and his fats. To Thomas, it felt as though he had been in a small hell which did not burn with fire but with darkness.

He went out and lingered for a while, before passing the three houses Ndosi had told him about. He coughed, but there was no Ndosi. He felt like shouting, but then the driver appeared from the dark, saying nothing, following Thomas. When they had covered some distance Ndosi asked: "What did Sihlangusinye say was wrong with your knee?"

"He gave me some muti to rub on it and said I should bandage the knee with it."

"All this time is just for muti to rub?"

"No. He also cut me with a razor, to bring out bad blood."

"He must have good eyes, this Sihlangusinye, to be able to vaccinate a person in such darkness – I saw how dark it was as you entered."

The driver said that and walked swiftly. It was late, and he had not told the boys where they were going. However, when they found them, they had made a fire, and were boiling water to cook the dry mealies for the road the next day, and they had also warmed the food. The two men sat down to eat and then slept. Never before had Thomas slept in a place where there was noise made by people who did not sleep at all. This noise combined with the sound of the sea not far away, the waves chasing and hitting each other. And further down you could hear steam boats sounding as if they were lost. Thomas did not sleep until morning had almost broken. When he finally fell asleep, he dreamt that he was falling into a river and was drowning, about to sink, when there came a man who tried to reach him, but before he could see if the man was able to save him, Thomas awoke. He was wet with sweat.

During the day the whites came looking for Minister Grout's oxen, and saw them. They loaded their luggage and pitched a tent on the wagon for shelter. The oxen were inspanned, and they all left for Mvoti. As it was late, the other wagons were quite far ahead by then. However, when night fell they had reached oThongathi. They outspanned the oxen, and the driver promised to watch them the whole night, so that Thomas and the boys could stay at the wagon and see to it that the ministers had an undisturbed sleep.

They again inspanned early in the morning, hoping to arrive at Mvoti just when the sun set. And Thomas was in a hurry, impatient to try the fat of that-which-comes-out-standing on Nomkhosi.

13

In Zululand, if young men wanted to know about a young woman of a certain area, they did not approach older people of that area to ask about her, lest they be given misleading information. The first thing they did was to get to know the boys of the area and then ask them: "Boys! Is there a young woman in that homestead?"

Then the boys would say: "Yes. It's not just one; there are many."

"But where do they live, as I never see them?" the "child of a young man" would say, leaning on his stick.

The boys would say: "How can you see them, as you are not from here? You should come here at such-and-such a time, and we will show them to you. They fetch wood from that forest; they fetch water from there; and as for bathing, they bathe in that ford."

"What are their names, friends?" The man would follow with his questions, while he knew the name of the young woman he was looking for. The boys would recite the names until they got to the name of the one he was looking for, and then he would say:

"So who is the boyfriend of so-and-so, my friends? Where are the young men who tend to stop her, and the children who keep visiting her?"

The boys did not understand what was good or bad, they just told their story: "The person you are asking about is engaged to a young man whose name is so-and-so. We never see her standing with another one. One day a certain young man tried to stop her against her will but she took him and threw him down and tied him to the grass."

Sometimes the boys would act as if this was *their* business, and while they were busy forming animals with clay, or herding, one of them would ask: "What did the young man do?"

"He struggled and struggled but could not free himself, until he called us, saying, 'You boys, come here.' And indeed we went. He said: 'Free me from this.' We freed him. And off he went; his sticks were taken by the girl who went to show them off at her home."

All the boys, who were a little naughty, laughed and said: "Awu, friend, do you think she can do like that to me?"

One would say: "Never." And all would burst out laughing. The inquiring stranger would be listening to all of this because he wanted to study the characters of the girls of that area. If a girl had a bad character, the boys would disagree about her: "She does stand with so-and-so from so-and-so." And the other would say: "She doesn't stand with him alone, she also stands with so-and-so." And the other would say: "So-and-so keeps asking me to call her for him."

No matter how the story had started, it always ended with the naughty boys joking about it, some even saying: "As for me, I would beat my sister up if she agreed to speak to all those scoundrels." And another: "Awu, men, is that a person at all?"

In the meantime, the inquiring stranger, having heard what he wanted, would simply disappear and the boys would not even notice.

One day the boys of Mzwangedwa were herding, and a man appeared and approached them. He asked about Makhwatha's daughters, starting with their leader, Nontula: "Tell me boys, what is the name of that grown girl of Makhwatha?"

"Which one? You mean the one who is the leader of all Makhwatha's daughters? Where are you from that you don't know that Nontula is going to be married to the Mkhwethus there at the royal house?" answered the boys.

The man said: "No, boys, I'm from far away. I heard that there was another who was found. To whom is she betrothed?" The boys were quiet for a while, until another suggested: "He is talking about Nomkhosi who lives at the minister's." Then one said: "That one we don't know, but she usually walks with the gentleman from the believers, escorting her. There is no one else she walks with."

"Damn it," said another boy, who was finishing the cow he was moulding from clay. "That young man from the white man's land – we don't understand him!"

The man's interest was aroused, so he moved closer to the boy, who was not aware of the impact of his words, having his eyes fixed on the clay cow he was moulding. He continued to perfect it, sometimes putting it down to inspect it. The man asked: "Why do you say so, my friend?"

"I'm saying that because always, when the sun is setting and we are separating the calves from their mothers, we see this young man entering Ntombinjani's house."

"Who is Ntombinjani, boy?"

Then from the side: "Ntombinjani is Nomkhosi's sister from a different house, but it seems she's having an affair with this young man who is betrothed to her sister."

"How do you see that, boy?"

"I see it with my eyes, because when he's leaving, Ntombinjani comes out with other girls to escort him, then in front of the homestead the other girls sit down, and the young man stands with Ntombinjani away from the others, discussing their own matters."

"And you don't know what they say, boys?" The man laughed, and the boys stood up as it was time to milk the cows. For the first time they took a close look at the man they were talking to: he was an older man, not a young man who was intending to court the girl.

"Why do you look at me like that? Have you never seen me before?" The boys kept quiet and moved further away from him.

"Awu, it's like I have seen you before. Are you not the one who drives the oxen of the minister, and I think I've seen you with this young man who is Ntombinjani's lover."

Then the man realised that the boys recognised him as Ndosi, the minister's driver. He filled his pipe and then left to check on the minister's oxen.

What did Ndosi want with Ntombinjani? Had he not been interested in her, he would have gone on to ask information about all the other girls in the Makhwatha household. Ndosi was a strong believer; he was married, had a happy home, disliked polygamy, and did not tolerate all the dark ways. So what did he want with Ntombinjani?

Before he left, Ndosi asked where Ntombinjani and her sisters fetched wood. The boys told him, and also told him the time when the girls normally went to the forest. When he arrived back at the minister's home, where he was living (his own home being rather far away), Ndosi sat down. He thought about talking to Nomkhosi but did not know how to get hold of her in private. He went to sleep thinking about this, and woke up to see Thomas preparing the wagon which was hauled by the two horses. Then suddenly he saw the minister and his wife getting on the wagon and Thomas driving for them. They were going to visit some believers some distance away. They were going to return in the afternoon. So Ndosi was not going to inspan that day.

When he saw that they were far away, Ndosi came closer to the minister's house and knocked. Nomkhosi answered: "Who is it?"

Ndosi said: "It's me, nkosazana." As he said that, the minister's children laughingly tumbled out of the door, their hair falling down over their heads. Ndosi also laughed and greeted them as

Nomkhosi came closer: "How can I help, Ndosi? Are you hungry? There's plenty of food in the house; the induna is away who would have shouted at you if he saw you eating here." She went back into the house and returned with a plate of food exuding an aroma that made one's mouth water.

Actually, Ndosi had eaten and was not at all hungry, but if he refused it, he would not be able to sit down with her, and listening to the little story he had come with would not be palatable to her. She gave him a spoon, took a chair for herself and sat, surrounded by the children, opposite him.

"We've been waiting a long time for your wedding, nkosazana, really; when are you getting married?"

"Me? I don't know, I'm waiting for my husband; he's the one who knows."

"No. That's not true. He, too, points at you, saying he's waiting for you."

"No. He's lying."

"I don't think so. You are the one who's having cold feet. Aren't you looking somewhere else, nkosazana? Even though my position here is lower than yours and requires that I respect you, I am in truth old enough to be your father."

"There's nothing more that I can tell you, except: I'm waiting for my husband."

"But let me, of the Ndosi clan, tell you clearly that the fault lies with you. You're running away from Thomas, and I wonder where you think you'll find another one like him."

Angrily Nomkhosi stood up, not wanting someone like Ndosi to talk to her like that.

"Is that how you thank me, Ndosi? I offer you food when you're hungry and now this is how you thank me?"

"No, nkosazana, don't be angry. I was not hungry at all."

"Then why did you eat my food?"

"I accepted it because I wanted to talk to you in private. Sit down, let's talk, and I will also finish the food you gave me," the minister's driver said, and took a spoonful, while the girl stood and watched this man who seemed so disrespectful to her. She was irritated, and folded her arms around her pinafore, watching him quietly.

"Sit down, nkosazana, otherwise all your matters will come to a standstill, as they are indeed standing still now."

"What do you mean by this?"

"I know that you are the fiancée of induna Thomas. On top of that, I also know that your heart is no longer content with him."

"How dare you say all this to me?" The girl's voice suddenly filled with tears. What Ndosi said hurt her; this thankless man who talked so carelessly to her – she who was respected by the workers of the minister, and by all the people of this area.

"No, nkosazana, I said sit down so I can talk to you, I'm an elder."

Nomkhosi sat down resentfully, the fury of an insulted woman aroused in her.

"I was in Durban with your future husband, and he asked me where Sihlangusinye lives. I was amazed to hear this as he's a trusted man who was on his first visit to Durban, but now the first thing he asks is for the diviner Sihlangusinye, and not the shops where they sell clothes and concertinas."

"I don't understand you, Ndosi. What are you saying?" Nomkhosi wiped her eyes and settled down in her chair like someone who wanted to listen.

"This is the truth."

"What's the truth?"

"I'm saying your husband went to Sihlangusinye."

"To Sihlangusinye's home? Really?"

"I went with him on these two feet, and I saw him with these two eyes. He entered alone, but since he forced me to escort him,

I waited until I saw that he was well inside, then followed him, tiptoeing until I could stand by the grass bundles and listened, because he told me that he was going to get herbal medicine for the knee he sprained when he fell from a horse."

"So it means he was looking for herbal medicine for his knee! Don't you know that he once fell from a horse? No. Stop right there! You're trying to breed enmity between me and Thomas. Shut up, I am leaving now." Nomkhosi stood up.

"I said sit down," started Ndosi, "this is why there is no progress in your relationship."

"Why should I sit here while you are speaking badly about a man who is going to be my husband? You are corrupting my ears. Did I send you to spy on him through bundles of grass?" Nomkhosi stood up, asked for the plate, called the minister's children, went inside and shut the door.

Ndosi felt like a fool. He thought Nomkhosi would want to hear about the bad things Thomas did in secret, but was surprised to see the girl standing up for her man, refusing to hear any unpalatable thing about her lover. He walked back wearily.

Once inside the house, faced by the children who knew nothing, the dishes, the beds, the pots cooking food on the fire, Nomkhosi came to her senses and regretted not listening to what Ndosi had to say about Thomas. Ndosi was not a talkative person, but today he had had the courage to speak to her. There was something between Thomas and Sihlangusinye, and she was clearly involved in this matter. She talked to herself, and indeed saw how her whole life was standing still. She went to her room and opened the kist: she saw the black silk handkerchief, she saw it announcing Nsikana and felt bad about Ndosi's words: "Sit down, this is why there is no progress in your relationship."

Meanwhile, Ndosi slowly walked back to his home and sat down to think, because he did not like Thomas. Thomas ill-treated all of them, he was cruel and was having an affair with Ntombinjani; he was lying to this girl who trusted him so much. But the worst was: he collaborated with sangomas who used evil potions while he was supposed to be a believer. What would the minister say about this? He found himself determined to see to it that this matter was the one that separated Thomas from Nomkhosi. But this separation would not be easy because the girl was committed to Thomas. Even if Thomas was serious about Nomkhosi and only playing with Ntombinjani, why would he go to search for love potions from Sihlangusinye?

Ndosi knew that Nsikana had managed once to talk to Nomkhosi, but did not know how far they had discussed things. He liked Nsikana. Whenever their paths crossed, they greeted each other. He often followed him with his ears, because this man was such a good musician, singing with his concertina his famous song: "Dida Nomasinga, you're lying to me." The young man was a believer, and always respectful. He decided to advise him to use that fat of that-which-comes-out-standing, at least; better that he did that and got Nomkhosi than for her to marry Thomas.

So as soon as he could, he met Nsikana on his way to Mvoti. While they walked together, Ndosi explained to him that perhaps the reason why the girl he loved did not accept him was because Thomas used the fat of that-which-comes-out-standing. When he said this, Nsikana, Bhoqo's son, let out a wild laugh and said: "I'm from Durban, my Father, those tricks I've long since heard about. How is it *possible* to think that the fat of a living person can bring you good? It may cause evil, but as to good, never. I refuse to believe that!"

"You are right, my child. You are right; I see that I'm at fault because we, as the believers, have our own God who will help us if we worship."

"Have you forgotten David's psalm: Even as I travel in the shadow of death I shall not fear evil?" Nsikana said while looking at the driver as if saying, "Your faith is still this small?"

Ndosi felt thwarted; when he tried to help people, they did not want to be helped. When he left Nsikana, he thought he had never seen such a stupid man! Wasn't Nsikana supposed to say, at least, that he, too, then, would find others to help him, so that when he met the young woman again, he would not be overwhelmed by bad luck? However, deep in his conscience Ndosi heard a voice saying: stand aside and watch, for you have not quite seen the power of the New God as explained by the ministers. Nsikana was so trustful of God that he would wait and see; wait and see the power of God in heaven and not the power of the ancestors as divined by diviners and sangomas.

Nsikana left Ndosi and headed straight to Mvoti to his friend, Nkomeni. "My friend," he said, "I have just met one who is like you. He also had sympathy for me regarding Nomkhosi. Is he not the minister's driver?"

Nkomeni answered: "Your rival is disliked by people, including those at the minister's home. All the minister's workers say he is cruel."

"The driver says I must be careful: I will not get the girl because my rival has left the faith and is now carrying Sihlangusinye's charms."

"You see! Didn't I tell you that it's good to use charms now and then? But you just laughed at me as if I am a fool."

"I rightly laughed at you! And even now I am laughing at you. I will only do these things of yours when I have lost all hope in everything I do on earth. Even if I lose Nomkhosi, I will go back to Durban and work for money, and take care of my sister and my mother, because my father abandoned them when they chose to become believers."

"Since you refuse to follow my advice, did you at least go to Makhwatha's and see Nontula?"

"Yes, I did."

"What did she say?"

"I saluted, and stayed at her mother's house as people had advised me. I asked for water and drank, and it was Nontula herself who gave me the water. After I drank I said I wanted to speak to her."

"Weren't you shivering?"

"Shivering? Who?"

"You! Who were you talking to, really?"

"I talked to her outside, and I told her all about my journey; but she didn't answer, just said yes, she hears me. She asked my name and the moment I said it, she laughed. That's how it ended." As his friend was equally nonplussed about Nontula's behaviour, Nsikana walked home, playing his concertina.

14

For the first time ever, Nontula visited Nomkhosi at the minister's

For the first time ever, Nontula visited Nomkhosi at the minister's home. She polished her head-ring and wore her skin-skirt made from a wildebeest that had come all the way from Zululand and been paid for by a black short-horned ox. She covered her chest with a shawl as a mark of respect, since she was going to the land of the white man; she properly arranged all the beadwork on her legs and arms, and rubbed herself with good-smelling perfumes. She walked with short, firm strides, carrying the short knobkierie her father had given her to use to look after the flock of girls at home. She did all this because she intended to spend the night with Nomkhosi. She left in the afternoon and arrived at sunset. She sat down to cool herself under the trees, and had food brought to her there. She ate there and only got up when it was time to sleep. That night Nomkhosi did not sleep in the minister's house; she slept with her sister in another house, and the children slept with their mother. Nontula made her bed on the floor, and Nomkhosi did the same, not wanting to look down on her elder sister.

That night they started to talk about Nomkhosi's engagement and coming wedding. Nontula came to the point: "Look, Nomkhosi, I don't have any problem with you marrying the Nogiyelas. I congratulate you. But I want you to cut your trees carefully because there's no road without potholes, my father's child. There's one thing I don't like, and it is to hear that our brother-in-law is saying good things about Ntombinjani. I spit on their relationship because it's suspicious to me."

"I hear, my father's child, but I trust Thomas so much that I don't think there is another person he thinks about other than me."

"I'm not going to argue with you, because you know Thomas better than I do; I only know him from a distance. In all my years, and you see how old I am, I know the world, Nomkhosi, and I know what young people are like when it comes to matters concerning the youth: sometimes they just ignore certain things if they don't want to engage in an argument."

"I also can't argue with you about this, because I know Thomas very well."

"Do you really know him?" said Nontula.

"I know him, really. No one can tell me anything about him."

"Even where he walks, you know that?"

"Yes, I know, my sister, it's true, I know him because he never goes anywhere. He gets off from work and goes to his house."

"If somebody came and said, 'Here Nomkhosi, Thomas said this and that about you,' and that he doesn't love you any more, wouldn't you believe it?"

"I wouldn't believe it because I know Thomas; that would be jealousy speaking, my sister."

"All right, then, light-complexioned maiden of my mother's house, you do trust Thomas, and I trust him like you do; let's leave that while we still stand and fall together."

"Where would I go if I was abandoned by you?"

When she heard Nontula snoring, Nomkhosi realised that sleep had taken her sister unawares. But she herself was unsettled; she had assumed that Nontula had come to tease her a little, but now she used the opportunity to rethink everything that Nontula had said. Indeed, it might be true. All the workers received their food from the minister's house, but lately Thomas almost always said that he was tired, wanted to eat early and go to his room. And then he left. Whether he truly went to his room to sleep, Nomkhosi did not know. What she did remember from earlier was that Thomas never needed a lot of sleep and always went to bed late; so why did he go so early these days? But Nomkhosi, too, was tired and soon fell into a deep sleep.

She dreamt that Nontula grew large in front of her, into somebody awe-inspiring. It was also as if she had long wings with soft feathers keeping the cold at bay. When she raised the wings, there appeared beneath them a handsome young man who came straight to Nomkhosi. She tried to step aside for him, but he came straight towards her. He was fearsome but had no evil about him. What amazed her was that no matter how she tried to step aside, he came straight at her, his eyes directed towards her. Nomkhosi awoke. She looked around the house and heard Nontula snoring, as she was still asleep. She turned over onto her side and again fell into a deep sleep. As soon as she was asleep, she had the same dream of Nontula's open wings releasing a young man walking straight towards her. When she woke a second time, she was drenched in sweat, from fear. She lay down again, and after a time she fell asleep and slept till morning.

Nontula woke up and returned home, leaving Nomkhosi a message that she would come back the day after tomorrow, and that Nomkhosi should expect her as she would not spend the night then. Nontula did come back, and she met with her sister at the river when Nomkhosi went to do the washing. They sat down on the rocks and talked.

"When I spoke with you the day before yesterday, I mentioned your husband's visits to Ntombinjani, but I saw that you didn't take it seriously."

"Indeed, things are not clear to me."

"Do you think that I, being as old as I am, would waste my time coming here to talk nonsense?" Nontula's voice sounded aggrieved.

"It's correct of me not to believe something like that, no matter from where it comes, because it tarnishes the name of a man I'm marrying."

"Marry if you want to marry, nobody cares about that, but take this from the mouth of Makhwatha: this foot of mine you will not see at your wedding if you respond to me with such rude words."

"I'm sorry, my sister. If I am angry, it's not against you, but against Ntombinjani who does this to me."

"What did *she* do to you? Have you ever seen her coming here to talk with your husband? Have you ever heard, even in Zululand, that a girl was keen on a young man and then pursued him to his home 'pretending to be eating grass' there? I don't know about the ways of the white man's land. And if it's like that, forgive me and let me die as I am, Makhwatha's daughter!" As she said this she hit a rock with her knobkierie, and then looked down into the water and saw herself as she was.

They went back together to Nomkhosi's room. She had taken her things from the kist and put them on the bed, where they found everything lying. Among the clothes was the secret handkerchief. Nontula recognised it from the words Nsikana had spoken to her.

"Nomkhosi, where did you get this expensive handkerchief? Tell me, and do not hide anything from me, because I am one of your own."

"Why do you want to know all that is in my heart?"

"It is law that you tell me. And I have the power to persist, to demand that you tell me, whether you like it or not. I don't want to use that power over you, but if you continue like this ... Look here, it's just the two of us here, talk to me!"

"If that is what you want, I'll tell you. This handkerchief came from a man who lives around Nkobongo, who fell for me when I was young."

"He fell for you when you were young; where did he see you?"

"I don't know. He said I should wait for him and he would see me when I was grown."

"So today you are not grown yet?"

"I'm grown."

"Have you met? What did you say to him?"

"We have not met. He went to Durban to work, but now has returned. I hear that he's around here. We have not met face to face but he once came here to talk to the minister, accompanied by his sister."

"What is the name of that man of yours?"

"No. He's not my man."

"I am asking the name of that man."

"He said to me he was Nsikana Mbokazi."

"I hear you, ntombi, but why did you accept the handkerchief? Here in the white man's land do young men give young women presents even before they accept them? That is a new way of courting!"

"I don't know if young men give presents to young women, but as for me, I accepted the handkerchief and was pleased with it."

"I see, Nomkhosi of my father; because you think that your knowledge of the white man's land gives you wisdom of the world. I know all about this matter of yours. Even its beginning when you were young, I know about it. And I know more than that, Nomkhosi."

"Oh. Such as ...?"

"Let me tell you. You remember one day when a man who wears skins came here and slept in the hut; who said he was going to Durban?"

159

"I remember, but there are many men who pass here; but yes, I remember that one. He was still a youth, tall and walking alone."

"You have said it."

"So. I remember him."

"Yes. He stopped and just had an informal conversation, this stranger."

"You know who it was?" Nomkhosi said this, and remembered that when she was talking with Thomas, this man kept coughing; and that the stranger praised her beauty in amazing words, words that she had never heard before; and that she felt his eyes in the dark fixed on her as he ate.

"Yes, I know. It was indeed Nsikana, running away from Nonoti where his brothers had conspired to have him killed. He cannot forget your kindness."

"Why did he hide himself like that?"

"All the hiding of himself, including the wearing of skins, was so that he could see you alone, and find out about you and Thomas. And indeed, he saw the two of you talking; he saw that indeed, you are in love."

"So you know."

"You see, it's because you think everything I say is just empty words. Didn't you say just the day before yesterday that you don't believe there is anything between Ntombinjani and this Thomas of yours; this man you worship as if he is the late Qwabe waking up to recite a poem at Nodwengu. Are there no other young men? As for me, I could tie up this Thomas with a rope and haul him here and that would be nothing to me; if that causes Maphahleni to rise, I don't care!

Nomkhosi was quiet, stunned by the fact that Nontula knew all these things, even tiny details.

"I know you're not a diviner, so how do you know all this?"

"Well, today I am. But if I am wrong about your story, then I'm not. Yes indeed, Nsikana is smart, this son of Mbokazi in Nkobongo! I have investigated his young manliness, and found it to be there: he's independent; he supports himself; he's indeed a good man."

"Oh, he made such a fool of me, digging out all my insides and leaving me an empty egg."

"Please, don't pretend that you're wise in the ways of this world, because you will fall and nobody will catch you."

"I'm done."

"Here's my advice: go and weave a piece of beadwork from blue and red beads, and put it on the knobkierie I hid there." They went together to a place where the grass stood high. At a clump of grass, Nontula bent down and brought out a new knobkierie made from a black peeled tree.

"I'm not going to tell you to accept Nsikana, or to reject him, or to continue with Thomas. But as a leader of all our father's young women, I'm betrothed to chief Mkhwethu of Mzwangedwa, as you know; so I am advising you, remember your promise to Nsikana, and Thomas's relationship with Ntombinjani of our own father. Take this knobkierie; I will come next week for it. You must welcome me on Wednesday afternoon under those lucky-bean trees near Wombe." They said their goodbyes and separated. Nontula went home, leaving Nomkhosi with the knobkierie in the minister's yard. Nomkhosi said nothing in response to what Nontula said, but was completely overwhelmed by the shadow she had left, and everything else.

During the night, she dreamt the same dream again, and whichever way she moved, she found the eyes of this young man were on her, engrossed, eating her like fire eating overgrown grass. It did not matter how the dream started, it ended with her waking up wet with sweat. She did not know what this meant. She went back to sleep. It came in a different way now; this young man appeared as another person, but she was not afraid because this person became Thomas. Nomkhosi was happy and said to him: "Why did you scare me so?"

Thomas said: "I wanted to hold you because I saw you were leaving me."

Nomkhosi said: "Leave you how, since I am dedicated to you?"

Thomas said: "I saw you leaving me, then I followed."

Nomkhosi woke up and tried to thrash out in her mind the things she had discussed with Nontula.

On the following Wednesday Nontula told Nsikana that Nomkhosi was going to meet her and he must follow in her footsteps, and pretend to be sauntering around "eating grass".

Nomkhosi was working with beads on the kierie, even though she did not know why she was doing so. Maybe it was her sister's gift to Chief Mkhwethu. She was smiling as she carried it to wait for her sister under the lucky-bean trees. She looked far away and saw herds of cattle grazing, scattered about, with no one looking after them. In front of her the grass was waist-high and sweeping green towards the horizon. It was falling this way and that way, blown by the summer wind from the sea. Some of the grass swished and sang when the wind touched it, like the roof of a house whispering till morning to the wind. Nomkhosi saw all this and was happy that she was still young; she was as green as the grass. She looked at the beautiful kierie and smiled again.

Nontula appeared, walking with short strides, using her stick as if she was tired. Nomkhosi stood up to meet her but Nontula waved her back: "Sit down, I'm coming there to the shade."

Nomkhosi did not sit down, but stood there holding the stick decorated in an exquisite design of blue and red beads. When she handed it to her sister, Nontula refused: "No, Nomkhosi, it's

162

not mine, it's yours because I gave it to you and you decorated it."
Nomkhosi laughed, feeling, in her mind, like a child.

As they were still talking, Thomas appeared, on his way from the minister's home to see his lover. He was startled when he suddenly saw Nomkhosi and Nontula. He knew that if Nontula ever knew about him and Ntombinjani, she would be his enemy forever. His guilty conscience made him scared of her; he knew that this daughter of Makhwatha was not afraid of any young man. Alarmed, Thomas waited, and then greeted them.

"Greetings to you of a great homestead."

"Yes, we see you, husband," said Nontula. "Are you going to visit us today across the Mvoti River?"

"No, I actually don't have time these days."

"Yes, you say it right, husband, because you visit those you visit, but not us. Those you want to see, you see them every day."

"You are confusing me in your speech; I don't understand you."

"You do hear, it's just that you don't want to understand. Perhaps you're afraid of this Nomkhosi I'm walking with. Well, I am also scared of her; it would be better if it was just the two of us, husband," Nontula said, and looked him in the eye without flinching.

At that precise moment Nsikana appeared, pretending to be going on his way. Nontula pretended that she was surprised, not expecting this meeting of rivals. Nsikana came closer, greeted them all, smiled and asked about their health. He also asked Preacher Thomas when he would come to their place to preach there. Thomas responded lamely. All this time, Nontula was watching her sister, who appeared to be confused and scared, and the two young men.

She smiled and said to Nomkhosi: "Yes, here it is happening now. You are giving me this stick, but now *I'm* telling you to give it to one of your courtiers as a gift from you. That is what we do in Zululand, so give it to me and I will give it to the one you want."

Nomkhosi, who was already stressed by the unexpected events, found herself suddenly consumed by a deep and anxious panic. Her heart beat faster; she had never thought it would all come this. Too terrified to speak, she looked down, and then slowly faced Nsikana. Her sister took the beaded kierie and placed it in Nsikana's hands. As she turned to leave, she said: "Mbokazi, here is your stick. Take it, may it always remind you of Nomkhosi, and may you be proud of it, 'No matter when'." Nontula had finished her job.

Notes

1   You-of-the-Reed, used to address a king; possibly a reference to the tradition that the original ancestor of the Zulu people emerged from reeds.

2   Umgungundlovane is where Greytown was later established in the 1850s.

3   A reference to Theophilus Shepstone, who served in the colonial government in Natal from 1845, and was Administrator of Native Affairs from 1853 to 1875. He set out the boundaries of Zulu reserves in the colony and had a system of ruling indirectly through Zulu chiefs who were loyal to him.

4   The "white Mbuyazis" were white people living among black people, adopting their lifestyle. They had been drawn in by Mbuyazi, King Mpande's second son, in an effort to strengthen Mbuyazi's campaign (against his half-brother, Cetshwayo) to be the heir to Zulu kingdom.

5   Theophilus Shepstone: see Note 3 above.

6   In historical accounts, John Dunn is remembered for having had many Zulu wives, with whom he fathered over 100 children.

7   A reference to a famous rescue mission, when Ndongeni and Dick King set off from Durban on horseback for Hini (Grahamstown), to tell the British that Durban had been besieged by Boer forces, and that they needed reinforcements.

Glossary

amasi sour thickened milk

believer someone who has converted to Christianity (see also *Kholwa*)

bhayi (ibhayi) a piece of cloth worn over the shoulders by a traditional Zulu woman

Bhiyafu the Bluff, Durban

central house a grandmother's house; this is built in a homestead even if the grandmother is no longer alive

dagga marijuana, cannabis

duiker a type of antelope

eBhayi at or to Port Elizabeth

Fanakalo a pidgin language; a very simplified language based mainly on isiZulu, isiXhosa, English and Afrikaans

hawu an expression of surprise

Hini Grahamstown

imitsha see *umtsha*

imvulamlomo literally mouth-opener; a payment made to begin negotiations for lobola

induna (plural izinduna) a headman; a leader; a man in a senior position appointed by a chief or king

inyanga a herbalist, a healer

isibongo (plural izibongo) a traditional dramatic form of oral poetry that typically includes praises, historical allusions, and sometimes veiled criticism of its subject and advice

isigekle a wedding dance

izinduna see induna

kaffir historically an extremely insulting term for black people

Khangela Congella, an area in Durban

Kholwa a believer, a person who has converted to Christianity

kierie short for knobkierie

knobkierie a stick with a knob at one end, often used as a weapon

left-hand wife a man's second wife, married after the right-hand wife

lobola bride-price, traditionally cattle and other livestock paid by a bridegroom to the family of his future wife

MaMlambo literally River Mother, a mythical snake-like creature with great power

Mvoti an area near the mouth of the Mvoti River

muti medicine

ndibilishi (indibilishi) a penny

Nduna see induna

nkosana the heir of a chief; the heir of an ordinary man; also used as a respectful way to address an employer or boss

nkosazana a chief's daughter; the first-born daughter of a senior wife; also used as a respectful way of addressing a woman

Nonhlevu a person who has converted to Christianity

ntombi (intombi) a girl or young woman of marriageable age

right-hand wife a man's first wife, the wife most senior in status

scotchman a two-shilling coin

second senior wife a man's third wife, linked to the right-hand wife; if the right-hand wife does not produce a male heir, a son of the second senior wife is in line to be the heir; her status may therefore be higher than that of the left-hand wife

tamba a dance

tokoloshe a troublesome creature in traditional beliefs, part dwarf-like human and part animal

ubusenga a wire bangle

ukugiya a warrior's dance

ukugqiza a dignified style of walking

ukuphalaza vomiting induced by taking a traditional medicine

umemulo a coming-of-age ceremony held when a young woman is ready for marriage

umtsha (plural imitsha) loin covering of hide, worn by men

uMvoti the Mvoti River (also referred to as the Mvoti)

About the translator

Nkosinathi Sithole

Nkosinathi Sithole was born in 1975 and grew up in Hlathikhulu near Estcourt, KwaZulu-Natal. He studied at the Universities of the Witwatersrand and KwaZulu-Natal, and has a PhD in English Studies. He has taught at universities in KwaZulu-Natal, and is currently an associate professor of Literature Studies and Creative Writing at the University of the Western Cape. Translation formed an important part of Sithole's postgraduate studies, which included the translation of  hymns and stories from isiZulu. His debut novel, *Hunger eats a man,* won the Barry Ronge Fiction Award in 2016.

To view the translators speaking about the Africa Pulse series, visit
www.youtube.com/oxfordsouthernafrica